MEND MY SOUL

JODY KAYE

Join Jody's mailing list for access to free books and exclusive first looks at new releases!
www.jodykaye.com/newsletter

GHOST PSYCHIC
MYSTERY ROMANCE

Fragments of the Past
Mend My Soul

Chapter One

Anson

I take my right hand off the steering wheel and reach across the console to place it on Rae Lee's leg. Her skirt has slid above her knee, tempting me with her soft skin. But the truth of the matter is, I crave any connection with her. The need to touch her, to care for her, is all-consuming.

"Are you considering taking advantage of this situation?" The corners of her lips tip up in the teasing smile I adore.

Her fingertips rise to the black mask covering her eyes. She touches the elastic matting her chin-length blonde hair.

"Take advantage? I'd never do that."

The highway in front of us is the recipient of my wolfish grin, but my palm skims up her warm thigh.

Beneath the fabric of her dress, my fingers graze her lace panties. Agitated, she groans similar to when my phone rings in the middle of the night and it's the precinct calling.

Now's not the time for us to get frisky, but I've wanted to hold Rae Lee since before we left the cramped quarters we're currently calling home. More than sexual desire, I'm driven by a surge of protectiveness that ramped up exiting the Brighton city limits. I'm also trying to stop my girlfriend from reading my mind—something I hope to fuck she'd tell me if she could do—and using sex as a distraction technique.

She moves my hand to her knee and lays hers on top of mine.

I take my eyes off the highway for a second to glimpse how exceptionally pretty she is without even trying. Her blue camp dress looked like a tent on the hanger. But on her, with the ties cinched at the waist, it fits her weekend style to a T. It has buttons down the front. Rae Lee in anything I can unwrap is a gift. It reminds me I was a lucky bastard the night we met when I took off her button-down shirt and trailed my lips over the swell of her breasts which had peeked out of the lacy blue bralette she was wearing.

I lift our joined hands and kiss her knuckles.

At the beginning of my investigative career, if anyone had told me I'd volunteer to drive a psychic to a crime scene, I'd have said no way.

Falling for a medium?

As a police detective, I might've suggested a 24-hour hold.

However, fifteen years after Pearl Tatton's

disappearance, her mother wanted to enlist a psychic to solve the case. Despite thinking the woman was grasping at straws, I agreed.

I initially shrugged off the leads Rae Lee provided for the Pearl Tatton case as insignificant and esoteric psychobabble. Of anyone, there was no way Rae Lee should have known the intricate details of the young girl's final hours that the Brighton Police Department hadn't uncovered during its initial investigation.

Except, once Rae Lee presented evidence there was something else out there—something other-wordly—she changed my mind, and there was no turning back.

The hidden clues she is capable of unearthing are truly remarkable and it was Rae Lee's skill that brought Mrs. Tatton the closure she needed.

Unaware of our personal connection, a local sheriff, at the edge of the Uwharrie National Forest, remembered reading a newspaper article mentioning Rae Lee's involvement in closing the Tatton case. He put the Investigative Services Branch agent, who was seeking a meet-up with the psychic who assisted Brighton PD, in touch with me.

This morning, we're traveling North Carolina Route 49 South on our way to meet the agent and discuss the case that falls under their jurisdiction.

The drawback of being a clairvoyant is the toll it takes on Rae Lee's body. She has long-term health problems. So, while I appreciate the agent wanting Rae Lee's help, I don't particularly like exposing my girlfriend to vulnerable situations. The last thing I'd consider is letting her consult on her own.

I haven't told Rae Lee anything about the law enforcement agency interested in her help, the people involved, or the potential crime. Not that she'd want to know. That's not her MO and it's another reason she's chosen to start wearing a mask.

I turn the car to the right, pulling into a gas station parking lot. The exterior gray-blue paint is peeling, but the parking lot is immaculate for a business out in the middle of nowhere. Not a candy wrapper, random soda can, or a used paper cup litters the ground. The tinted doors gleam in the sunlight free of fingerprints smudging the glass behind the handles.

"Are we there?" Rae Lee folds her hands in her lap.

"Pit stop. Will you be okay while I'm in the convenience store?" I roll down the windows to give her some air and cut the engine.

"How many living people are outside?" Rae Lee asks.

"One male between eighteen and twenty-two. He's getting into a construction truck, carrying a bottle of Mountain Dew and a wrapped danish. Another, approximately forty, just pushed the convenience store door open and is making his way to a late-model red hybrid."

"What did he buy?"

"Coffee. He burned his mouth on the first sip."

"There's a cautionary tale," she teases me.

"Okay, smarty. How many dead people are here?"

Although wearing a mask is new for Rae Lee, our back-and-forth in these circumstances is normal.

"Three." She sighs. "One is at my window."

"Are they going to make trouble?"

Rae Lee turns her face toward the apparition she senses. "You won't make trouble, will you? I have a busy day ahead." She waits a beat before turning the discussion back to me. "Go on and refill your coffee. That's why we stopped, isn't it? Your travel mug is empty."

I chuckle under my breath. When I was a rookie cop, I used caffeine to keep me awake during overnight investigations. Nowadays, the constant low-dose drip in my system eases my nerves and keeps me focused.

"Want anything?" I ask.

"A sip of the water you'll use to cool it off."

My seat belt retracts, and I tug the car door handle. "How do you know I'm getting water?"

Rae Lee doesn't see into the future. Not that I'm aware of, anyway. Though right about now, that information might prove useful.

"Because, Detective Ames, the last time we stopped for coffee, it was too hot. You spilled an inch from the cup onto the sidewalk and poured in water from my cold bottle." Her nose wrinkles. "Please don't do that again. I think the owner tries to keep this place tidy, and they won't appreciate other customers tracking sticky coffee shoe prints into the store after walking through a brown puddle."

"Why do you say that?" Rae Lee can't see anything from behind her mask.

"We're parked right outside the building, not over by the pumps, and I can smell faint ammonia."

A grin pulls at my mouth. "I love you, you know that?"

I've grown to accept how in tune Rae Lee is with her world. But the fact that she uses her other senses —the skills I've honed after a decade on the police force—to stay alert never ceases to amaze me.

"I do." Her lips part, and she flashes me her teeth.

I'd lean over and kiss her, but we have the briefest chance for a pit stop or we'll be late.

Entering the gas station, the first things that catch my attention are a roll of paper towels and a three-quarters-full spray bottle of blue window cleaner on the counter in front of the lottery ticket display stand.

Homing in on the tall carafes, I make my way to the coffee bar. I twist the lid off my travel mug and hold it upside down to stop any condensation from dripping onto the clean station. Out of habit, I empty a single sugar packet in. Doing it makes me more approachable during interviews, more than I enjoy taste. Pressing on the coffee dispenser lever is second nature to me. I know how many times it will fill the cup without it overflowing. I turn my body, pretending to observe my sleeping girlfriend in the front seat of my car.

In my peripheral vision, a middle-aged man behind the counter snaps the white tape from the cash register. He moves to the main floor. A pregnant woman, on the younger side to become a mother, leans a mop and bucket against the wall nearby. As one enters the space, the other exits. The man's shoulder bumps the woman's.

"Don't leave that there," the man grumbles, as if he's told her one too many times.

He lumbers between the aisles and disappears into a back room, closing the door that reads: *Employees Only*.

The woman continues past him, unspeaking. I expect an uncontrolled eye roll from her or something to indicate her annoyance with his harsh demand. She just rubs her shoulder, like getting upset isn't worth the effort. She collects some trash and tosses it into a receptacle. Then, not allowing her burgeoning belly to get in the way, she reaches for the bottle of window cleaner.

Since no one else is in the store, I leave my cup on the coffee bar and walk over to the refrigerator cases for that bottle of water Rae Lee predicted I'd get. When I've cracked the cap and have finished making my cup of Joe immediately drinkable, I secure the lids on both beverages, toss my garbage, and approach the counter.

Meanwhile, the young woman has brought the mop, bucket, and other cleaning products to a small utility closet near the room the man went into.

"I'm sorry to keep you waiting." She waddle-hustles back, holding her stomach and dodging slick spots on the worn tiles.

"Not a problem. I'm happy to have fresh coffee for the last leg of my drive. Did you just make this pot?" I place the water and the cup on the counter.

"Right before you came in," she replies.

The worry lines someone her age shouldn't have

yet fade, as if I've given her a compliment. She pumps a hand sanitizer into her palm and rubs her hands together before scanning the bottle and a UPC on the register for the correct size coffee refill.

I absently wonder what sort of predicament a pregnant, not-quite-twenty-year-old girl has gotten herself into that custodial work and running the register at this convenience store is her best option. If I mention this encounter to Rae Lee, she'll laugh. Not at the young woman's circumstances. More that I need to practice shutting down my suspicious mind the way she consistently works to keep her barriers with the dearly departed in place.

I pull my wallet out of my back pocket to pay the cashier and notice she's regarding the stretch of my button-down over my biceps, the way I catch Rae Lee appreciatively looking at me when I get out of the shower.

A faint whirring hums through the air. Her shoulders stiffen and her smile falters. She bites her lip, tucks her long, wavy dark hair behind her ear, and darts her eyes to the *Employees Only* door. The man is monitoring her every move on closed-circuit television.

____

Chapter Two

Rae Lee

What are you talking about? I think.

Saying it out loud would open another can of worms.

The haggard woman outside my window with a cleaning cloth gripped in her fist is the source of the ammonia smell. She knows I can see her because she swore to me before Anson got out of the car that she wouldn't cause a problem.

I haven't paid close attention to the images she keeps flashing at me. The order rotates, but it's like she's talking in circles and the projection won't stop. A single-wide. Pinewood State. Ragweed. Someone sweeping away a hornet's nest.

I wish she were as quiet as the cold man huddled by the building. Even if I can't see him, he gives me the chills. The last person I sense comes and goes. They don't belong here, and my best guess is they were a motorist who died on this road.

The woman is forty-ish. I have an awareness of her as a living person. Her cheeks are full, and rings dig a groove in the fat finger on her left hand. When people appear to me looking like this, it's a sign her death was abrupt. Her nondescript clothes prevent me from telling how long ago that was. Whatever she wants to communicate is important to her. But that's almost always the case for anyone who sticks around after they've died—Angeline notwithstanding.

Anson's former partner was killed in the line of duty. They'd started a romantic relationship before her death, but I don't believe it's the reason Angeline hasn't crossed over. Her presence, though not meddlesome, is problematic for us.

It's not an ideal strategy, but thinking about her knocks the other woman's intrusive thoughts from my mind. I'm not summoning her. Angeline has her usual haunts; Anson's apartment, her mother Delores's house, and the baseball field where her son Grant plays ball. Even though she died a decorated detective, she won't follow us on an investigation.

I use the slip of silence to continue to quiet my mind and figure out where I am. Truthfully, I think human instinct is why I'm doing it. Like if a kidnapper threw me into the back of a windowless van, I'd sift through everyplace I've driven, hoping to sort out what road I was on to increase the possibility I could tell the authorities where they could find me.

Anson and I got in the car about an hour ago. Despite the frequent *tick-tick* of the directional as

Anson shifted between lanes, we took exactly one turn before he pulled the car into the gas station parking lot.

The sun was shining when we left home. Heat seeps through the windshield. I'm glad I rolled the window down or I'd suffocate.

Unlike the moldy cheese stench that the gas station Anson fills the car up at has on trash day, the scent is earthy with a pinch of spice. Outside of the major cities, North Carolina is agricultural. It smells like something is decomposing near where farmers raise hogs and chickens. We can't be there.

I take a deep breath, trying to suss out if we're west or south of Raleigh. The other option is east. But closer to the coast, the inlets reek of sulfur and algae. This air is too clean.

The woman shows me ragweed again. My nose tingles, and I sneeze.

Thanks for that, I want to say.

I pat around inside the center console for a tissue, finding a bumpy stack of fast food napkins. When I wipe my nose, I'm tempted to remove my mask. Am I surrounded by farm fields? Forest?

The longer I sit here, the more my experiment, dulling my sense of sight to see if it heightens my perception, annoys me.

At the onset, Anson was against blinding myself for any reason. He's a cop with his head on a swivel twenty-four seven. So, I expected his reaction. I swore having my eyes covered was strictly for driving to a crime scene or meeting with another investigator. He finally agreed doing it on the way prohibits me from jumping to conclusions and making assumptions about my environment before we get there. However, Anson limited me to wearing the mask in his presence.

I went along with my boyfriend's be-aware-of-your-surroundings speech because there were bound to be circumstances when he'd get out of the car. Eventually, he'll see the blackout mask has other benefits. I haven't quite gotten the nerve to suggest to my safety monitor that I wear the mask at home in bed… When we're not asleep.

I sigh, bored, and wondering how much longer this pit stop will take. Since I don't know where we're going, our conversations have been stilted. The life we're building together isn't always this serious. After this consultation, we're actually on vacation. Weirdly, though, Anson's changed the subject whenever I've started talking about that. He'd prefer I focus my energy on the meeting. Another reason I'm ready to get there and get to work.

A woodpecker pecks, and I smile.

Forest.

The convenience store door swings open. Then the car door. I smell Anson's cologne and hear the thunk of the metal travel mug into the cupholder, followed by the water bottle.

"Miss me?" The retractor for his seat belt zips, and he clicks it into place.

"Terribly." I reach for the water bottle.

I'm not thirsty. I need something to fidget with, or

else I'll wring the skin off my hands soon. Aside from being tight-lipped about who we're meeting, I feel like Anson's holding other cards close to his chest. We don't keep secrets from one another. Recognizing something is up is throwing me for a loop.

"How much further?"

"We're almost there."

Twenty minutes later, we turn off the main road. I can feel the car sway as Anson attempts to avoid potholes. Nevertheless, I bounce in my seat. The heat radiating through the windows dissipates. I rub my arms, then fumble with the vent, flicking the air away from me. When the car stops, I hear the crunch of earth underneath the tires.

"We're here," he tells me.

I lift the mask.

"Wait. Gimme a sense of what you think you know," he instructs.

I sit back in the passenger seat, pulling together the clues I've collected along the way, venturing a guess

"The air smells like pine trees, and the last mile of road wasn't well maintained. The car hasn't slowed for traffic, so we can't have gone as far as Charlotte— Wait, is that a boat?"

I hear an outboard motor and push up my mask.

We're in an unpaved section of the parking lot for a boat ramp. There are empty boat trailers and a speedboat puttering in the clearing next to a concrete dock. The driver of the truck it's launched from pulls the truck and trailer past us.

I turn to Anson. He's got a lopsided grin on his face

that says he's proud of me. Although I relied on four of my five senses instead of any psychic abilities for what I got right. I could have blindfolded him, and he'd have come to the same conclusion.

Blindfolded. Hmm... I think, not for the first time, looking at my boyfriend. His laugh lines mean he's had a mostly good life. The fine premature gray strands of hair mean his job as a police detective takes its toll. He's dressed in a collared shirt and khaki pants with a crisp crease that he ironed barefoot this morning, wearing tight boxer briefs, a St. Rita medal around his neck, and nothing else.

He also ironed my dress, earning bonus blow job points, because I'd rather scrub the floor with a toothbrush than iron.

I stuff my oversexed thoughts to the back of my mind. I can gawk at Anson at the hotel later on.

Getting out of the car, we're met by a female agent. Her auburn hair hangs over her shoulder in a braid. Her ensemble is typical of law enforcement: a brownish-gray shirt and khaki pants with utility pockets. She's of average height, but bulky. Although I think the clothes detract from her true body type. After a moment, I register the national parks patch embroidered on her sleeve.

"Anson Ames?" She reaches out to shake his hand.

"Agent Reed, nice to meet you. This is Rae Lee Chatham."

"Rae Lee, call me Moira. I don't know the correct protocol for this. Am I allowed to touch you?"

"Shaking hands won't affect what I see and I

promise I won't read your mind."

"Can you do that?" Moira grips my palm, laughing uncomfortably.

"Not at all... So, um, this is a pretty site. Are we going for a boat ride?"

"Unfortunately, no. Our victim was found nearby and ISB was hoping you could provide some insight?"

"I'll try my best. Do you mind if I walk around a bit to get my bearings?"

"We'll stay out of your way," she agrees.

I'm drawn toward the boat launch. The speed boat I heard has moved downstream. Water laps at the cement dock. I stand at the end. My eyes scan the opposite side of the reservoir. This is a busy place and I feel motion all around me; laughter and the lingering frustration of boaters angry that something has gone wrong with their boat during their day on the water.

The problem is, that's the only negativity I sense. Any death is unaccompanied by trauma. When no particular scenario presents itself, I decide the residual energy is from fishermen whose families have scattered their ashes in the lake.

And that fills me with dread. Whomever Agent Moira Reed asked me to look for has moved on. I don't get the faintest impression they were here. Not to mention, any normal person can deduce a large body of water likely means she's investigating a drowning.

Unless the cops found the victim in the woods? But there's really nowhere to hide a body near the parking lot. I'd also suspect Agent Reed would have more evidence if that were the case.

Then again, what I've gleaned about criminal cases comes from having a cop as a boyfriend. Before we met, I had less than a handful of experiences working with detectives to solve cold cases. In addition, I'd put to rest playing psychic medium for friends who wanted me to contact their loved ones who crossed over because it was affecting my health.

I sit, tucking my dress under my bottom, and dangling my feet off of the dock. The water is a long way down. I picture myself with Layla. My best friend and I are holding hands. We're happy. Joking around about jumping. She encourages me to take a leap. When I do, I fall back into the water with my arms and legs stretched like a starfish.

I hit the water in a reverse belly flop. I twist my shoulders, seeking a reprieve from the phantom sting that pushes me out of musing. Invisible bugs skitter up my spine the way I get creeped out watching someone accidentally cutting off a finger in a gory movie. Just because the deceased show me all manners of death doesn't mean I enjoy it.

I straighten my back and adjust my sluggish hips. I've been stationary too long. Daydreaming isn't an effective use of my time. It's not why Agent Reed invited me here. If I don't stand up and report back to her, she'll think something is wrong.

Something is wrong.

Aside from the fact that I spent almost two hours blindfolded, it bothers me that there are no spirits lingering at this site. Most law enforcement, even the ones who are cautiously optimistic when they contact Anson, are also skeptical of my abilities. So going into this, I was worried that whoever we were meeting was already suspicious of me. Except now I'm concerned about how not finding anything useful will affect Anson's reputation.

I sigh deeply, like when I had pneumonia, and it was hard to breathe and get up to break the news that I uncovered zero clues to help solve the case.

Chapter Three

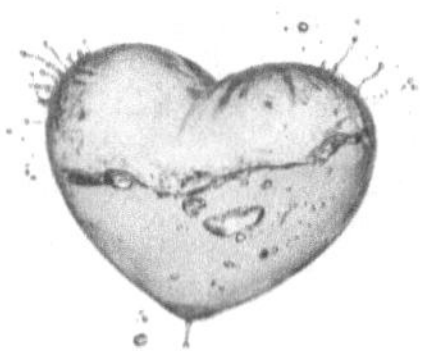

Anson

Rae Lee turns her back, walking toward the water's edge. Neither myself nor Agent Reed have given her anything to go on other than the victim was found here. So, if Rae Lee is drawn to the water, it's not because of the spectacular view. I'm confident she senses something.

"What can you tell me about the victim?" I ask Agent Reed.

Moira gave me a high level explanation over the phone after I assured the ISB Agent I never share any details with Rae Lee about the cases she's asked to consult on. While Rae Lee familiarizes herself with the location, We might as well review the details again.

"Xavier Martin. Age twenty. A fisherman spotted his body on the riverbank as the sun was coming up. Near as we can figure, the boat launch stopped it from moving further down river, but we're still uncertain how far downstream the body traveled."

"Any chance he was pushed?"

"Possibly." She slips her hand into her pocket. "Autopsy showed a skull fracture likely rendered him unconscious. The presence of water in the lungs drew the medical examiner to conclude the victim died by drowning.

"So he was alive when he went into the water. What's the riverbed like?"

"Upstream is exposed rock until springtime. The Army Corps of Engineers dug this section for flood control. The postmortem report included lacerations to exposed skin on the head, neck, and hands; contusions to the shoulders and legs. All injuries were consistent with the current carrying the submerged remains downstream."

"That's what I was afraid you'd say. Xavier Martin could've hit his head on a rock, or been hit over the head and dumped." I'm sure Agent Reed has pondered this. "How long was he in the drink?"

"Approximately three days."

If there was a struggle, any evidence underneath the fingernails was compromised by the water before resurfacing. Damn.

"Toxicology?"

I watch Rae Lee take a seat at the end of the dock. She stares down into the water.

"Negative for drugs and alcohol. And before you ask," Moira interrupts my stream of thought, "there's a bridge over the river about five miles upstream.

According to the locals, the water level the last day anyone saw Xavier was low. Larger rocks could've been a few inches underneath the water. There was heavy rainfall the day before the body washed ashore, possibly transporting the deceased from where they were injured to the boat ramp."

I noted the video monitoring sign by the entrance to the ramp, but suppose there's little chance of surveillance cameras outside this area.

I scrub my face, frustrated for the agent. "Nobody reported this kid missing?"

"Nope. When he didn't show up for his shift, his boss thought he quit." Moira shrugs. "The guy didn't know anything was amiss until we told him."

I recognize her head shake, and her expression. I've worn it myself, trying to figure out how people can discount other's situations, especially if there's any sort of animosity. Which it sounds like there was if the boss expected Xavier Martin to quit without giving notice.

"Parents?" Family? Didn't anyone care or try to contact him over those three days?

"Deceased. Martin lived alone. A co-worker said he moved a teardrop trailer from one wooded area to the next. He couldn't afford campground fees or parking tickets. To make matters worse, a group of three fourteen-year-olds committed a string of arson."

"Lemme guess—"

"Don't bother." She pulls up a photo on her phone of a charred camper. A forensic team couldn't pull prints from the burned-out shell if they tried. "We've had it stored in an evidence trailer for months."

I blow out a deep breath. "And I wondered why you were desperate enough to call in a psychic."

"Not cold enough for a cold case, Detective Ames?" she laughs. "All of my leads ran dry months ago. What do I have to lose?"

As I give Agent Reed her phone back, Rae Lee is getting up. She approaches us, her hands cupping her elbows. A sure sign something is bothering her.

"Anything?" I ask.

I'm setting the bar low for Moira. It's not like Rae Lee to walk away from an investigation with no impressions of the crime.

Hell, I've watched this woman run out of restaurants when another diner has brought an unexpected guest along with them, who recognizes Rae Lee's talent and won't leave her alone.

"I'm sorry. The person you're investigating isn't here. Not by the water, anyway."

Moira frowns.

"You got no other impressions?" I prod.

Taking out a digital recorder, I gesture to confirm with Agent Reed that she's okay with me recording the conversation.

"I received a lot of residual energy, but nothing jumped out at me, and no one approached me to speak. Not even a boater or fisherman who might've come here a lot when they were alive, and wanted to show me how special it was to them. Excuse me if my assumption is wrong, Agent Reed. But if you found your victim here, I doubt they had a connection to this place."

"I feel silly asking this, but would their spirit go elsewhere?" Moira inquires.

"Absolutely. They may go home, or some place important to them during their lifetime. They may also attach themselves to a loved one, or sometimes a not-so-loved-one?" Rae Lee's shoulder bounces.

"Like a haunting?" Moira blanches.

"Yes," Rae Lee replies, matter of fact.

Moira looks at me as if to say, *What good does that do if I don't know if anyone pushed Xavier?*

I blow out a breath, because I can't agree more. If the kid fell, he wouldn't be out for retribution. Not unless someone was unkind to him in life.

"Do you happen to have anything of the deceased's?" No different than Moira, Rae Lee is grasping at straws.

"I watched a show about people with abilities touching objects, otherwise I wouldn't have thought to check this out of the evidence locker." Moira opens her shirt pocket and removes a small plastic bag. Inside is a delicate bracelet.

"Can I take it out of the bag?"

Moira agrees, dumping the gold chain into Rae Lee's palm.

Rae Lee folds her fingers over it, closing her eyes.

"This belonged to someone who died, but the last person it belonged to wasn't the original owner. It's a cherished possession. I can feel a strong connection... A string connecting two hearts... And a feeling of... Hope?" A sunny smile breaks over Rae Lee's face and she tilts her chin toward the sky. "Like things can only get better."

Unfortunately, they didn't for the victim.

"Anything else?" Moira needs more to go on.

"An X." Rae Lee pauses. Her brows move up and down to decipher what it means. "Xander?"

Xavier.

"And three. There were three people this belonged to, but only two have a solid imprint on it."

"Why?"

"The last person didn't own it long enough."

"How do you know?"

"I have a jewelry business, Agent Reed. I create and sell necklaces and other trinkets to boutiques. The stones I use have healing properties." Rae Lee lifts the vibrant orange sunstone pendant wrapped in silver wire that hangs around her neck. "The energy is bi-directional. The easiest explanation is the wearer gets the benefits of the stone. The stone absorbs, or reflects, negativity from the wearer. Don't get me wrong, it can also absorb the good stuff. Happy feelings, sentiments, love."

"May I?" I interrupt Rae Lee, returning the dainty bracelet to Agent Reed.

While Rae Lee and Moira discuss the properties of gemstones, minerals, and other inanimate objects, I inspect the 14K engraving on the broken clasp, and then the intricate double links covered by tiny gold hearts. While Rae Lee is designing pieces she has cautioned me about how easily intricate jewelry is damaged. I'm curious how several of the fragile hearts got bent. However, I can't risk asking now, in case it leads my medium to any conclusions.

"It's very pretty, isn't it, Anson?" Rae Lee surprises me by asking.

The piece of jewelry is outdated by a good thirty years, and not my girlfriend's usual style. She wouldn't wear something like this.

I pop the bracelet into the evidence bag Moira is holding open.

"You're certain a third person owned it?" I'm confused about the imprinting.

"You know I hate it when you ask me for certainties. Cold, hard facts are your realm." Rae Lee's nose wrinkles and her lips twist. She thinks before she speaks again. "I can only tell you I got the impression the second person who had it and passed it on was optimistic. Giving it away was like a new beginning for them."

"Do you know if the giver was male or female?"

"Can I see it again?"

As soon as it's in Rae Lee's sight she blurts, "Male. Definitely male. I'm sorry, Moira. I wish I uncovered more for you to go on," Rae Lee apologizes.

"Honestly, I wasn't sure what to expect, but I know it wasn't that you'd solve this case. Thank you for your time, though. I appreciate your willingness to make a detour at the beginning of your vacation."

"It wasn't so far out of our way," I reply.

If anything else comes to you—" Moira gives Rae Lee her business card.

Rae Lee assures her she will.

The agent is grateful I intend to send her the audio recording of her discussion with Rae Lee, so she can review it once we're back from our trip. We separate. Rae Lee and I get back into the car to continue our drive south.

I read Rae Lee's body language when she crumples her mask, tossing it in the backseat. *So much for that.*

Thirty minutes later, she remains quiet.

"Wanna talk about it?"

"Not really," she starts, leaning her elbow on the window and her forehead in her hand. "I wish I were of more help."

"I know you do."

"Why weren't there enough pieces? Why didn't any more come to me?" She chuffs. "How could I have not seen anything, Anson? Do you know how hard I have to concentrate to keep everyone out?"

"Yes."

She covers her lips with her pinky. "Is it insane that, at a peaceful reservoir boat slip, I experienced exactly what I'd want to at a peaceful reservoir boat slip? Why am I complaining when plenty of times I'd give my right leg for a few hours as a normal person?"

"It's not complaining, in my book, when what happened was unexpected. Out of the norm."

Rae Lee is used to putting up with a lot of bullshit from people who should've followed the light.

"Do you think Agent Reed thinks I'm a phony? What if a different medium has the answers, but because I found nothing on my walk, she won't trust a second opinion?"

"Slow down. You are the second opinion." I rub her knee. "Moira's disappointed because she hasn't been able to solve a case. That's hard for an investigator. But when we left, I didn't get the impression she regretted calling in a psychic, or that seeking your help wasn't worthwhile. Remember, I'm the one who thought you were full of shit, *Raleigh*." I flash my girlfriend a smile, wink, and add, "In my humble opinion, your intuition hasn't led you wrong yet."

Rae Lee sighs, rolling her eyes. The corner of her lip tips up, and I'm assured Rae Lee just needed to blow off steam.

Sometimes, I bring the stress of police work home. Except, I can't imagine how hard it is for someone who can't disconnect from whatever bothers them. I almost canceled our reservations for this weekend, and found somewhere else to take Rae Lee, because I worried she wouldn't be able to get away on a historic getaway.

"I love you," I remind her.

"Love you, too." She sits up, leaning over to peck my cheek.

"And you have Agent Reed's card if you think of anything in the interim."

"I'd prefer to focus on having fun with you on vacation now instead."

"That's the spirit."

Chapter Four

Rae Lee

I brush away the lock of hair that's fallen across my forehead. Looking out the windshield, I can't believe my eyes. The brick hotel, at the center of the historic district, where we are staying, is six stories tall, with an impressive circular drive.

Around the time of our first anniversary, Anson asked if there was anything special I'd like to do to celebrate one year of dating. Together, we decided on a long weekend in Charleston.

Although this getaway is after our official first date —which happened at Mark-39 when Anson took me out to dinner to go over more about what I'd sensed about Pearl during my walk through at her childhood home, not when I gave him a false name and hooked up with him at Sweet Caroline's music hall—I'm still excited for it.

More so when Anson said part of my gift was if I

made a list of places I wanted to see, and restaurants I wanted to try, he'd plan everything else.

So, it's not as if I expected he'd booked us at the no-tell motel. But this hotel? Next level.

We get out of the car under a portico. Thankfully, rain isn't included in the weatherman's predictions. This weekend is supposed to be beautiful. Sunny with light breezes coming from the harbor.

Before the car comes to a stop, we're approached by two valets and a bellhop. In perfect coordination, one valet opens my car door, the other takes the keys from Anson, and the bellhop pops the trunk and removes our luggage. The second valet gestures for us to *come this way*.

Anson grabs my hand, lacing our fingers together. The reflective lobby doors open like magic and the bellhop pushes the suitcases behind us on a brass bellman's cart inside.

Anson checks at the front desk. The concierge gives him the keys to our room, and up we go in an elevator with an honest-to-god lift girl. Her outfit is complete with an adorable usher hat.

My cheeks bunch. This is extravagant. Almost an out-of-body experience. I'm tempted to ask my boyfriend to pinch me.

The bellhop requests the key card from Anson. They open the door for us and place our bags on the plush carpet.

I walk into the suite. If my jaw could drop lower, it would. I press my fingertips to cover my absolute awe. Then I spin toward my boyfriend, who is tipping the bellhop.

"Ohmigod, Anson. This place has more room than our apartment! It's amazing."

It's *just* a single room with a massive four-poster bed…and a king-size mattress…two cozy reading chairs…a long marble-top dresser…and a Juliet balcony that overlooks a charming street below. But when I couldn't take any more of Angeline's incessant hovering at his place, I asked Layla and Julian if the loft I'd rented from them was still available, and moved back into their home. Anson didn't hesitate to follow me. Along with Fred, the orange kitten he gave me, we've been squeezed into less than six hundred square feet of living space.

He smirks, shuffling closer. "A hotel should be better than what you're used to. If not, why would anyone want to go on vacation?"

"I'm not sure I'll want to go home after this."

"You will. By the end of the weekend, I bet you won't be able to wait to tell Layla every last detail," he says of my best friend.

I lift my arms over my head, and fall back onto the luxurious bed. About to sink into the fluffy softness, my memory jogs, and I glimpse myself starfishing off of the boat ramp into the water.

I'm certain Anson doesn't notice how fast I sit up and shake myself until he sits next to me, popping off a shoe.

"Are you feeling better than before?" he asks.

"Much. Thank you."

Anson's not as uptight as he was when we started

packing for this trip either, and that makes me deliriously happy. I don't want any silly squabbles coming between us and ending our vacation on a sour note.

I turn his face, cup his cheek, and kiss his lips tenderly.

Out of the corner of my eye, I spy a vase filled with colorful roses, lilies, and wildflowers on the writing desk. Next to the flowers is a tray of four of the largest chocolate-covered strawberries I've ever seen, covered by a glass cloche.

My mouth waters. We stopped for lunch hours ago.

"Is that for us?" I point. "Can we eat them now?"

"No, it's to keep any tagalongs happy. Yes, it's for us."

I squeal, throw my arms around Anson's neck, then jog across the room, lifting the dome. I bite into a juicy strawberry. It's massive, two or three bites, and so sweet, I think I've died and gone to heaven. Holding the stem, I bring it over for Anson to sample.

Pulling the hem of my skirt up with my opposite hand, I straddle his lap. Anson chomps a section off. Juice dribbles down his chin. He uses a knuckle to brush it off.

"I could have cleaned that up for you," I tease, removing the green leaves.

"Oh yeah? How about one more bite then?"

I pop the rest of the strawberry into his mouth. He grabs my fingers, sucking the juice from each one. The curl of his tongue makes my nipples pebble in my bra.

That wasn't what was supposed to happen, but your girl's not criticizing. Anson and I both want the same thing. How we get there doesn't make a difference as long as we get there.

He drags his finger over my lower lip, and I lick the wetness away.

"I didn't think I'd ever encounter someone as special as you are, Raleigh," Anson says.

I blush when he uses his nickname for me. The name I gave him when I was hoping against hope the broad chested guy with thick eyelashes who I picked up at a bar wasn't the police detective who had contacted me to consult on a case the next day.

From the moment we met, I've been drawn to Anson. I can blame it on how sexy he is, or the itch I needed him to scratch that night. But giving into my libido risked my reputation, and worse, I risked Anson's boss, Chaim, and other officers at the precinct treating him with disrespect for bringing a medium into their midst.

I'm lucky the stars aligned, and what we uncovered led to far more than one night in his bed.

Anson tucks a lock of my hair behind my ear and drags my lips toward his. His tongue swipes my seam and I open for him. He tastes of velvety chocolate and syrupy berries. I moan, starved for more than the delicacies on the plate. In return, he groans, fusing our mouths together.

My hips rock against the growing bulge behind his zipper. Anson uses one hand to hold me down as he grinds up. Dampness soaks my panties.

He tucks his nose to my neck, trailing kisses over my clavicle. When the fabric of my shirt impedes him from going any further, he grabs the sides, and rips it over my head.

My hands land on the broadcloth of his button-down. My chest rises and falls in sharp pants. My breasts swell over the cups of my bra. Looking at me with a dark gleam in his eyes, Anson skims a thumb over my taut nipple. Then he deftly flicks the clasp, freeing my breasts.

"Do you know how fucking hard you made me the first time, Raleigh? With your skirt around your waist like this, and your perky little tits begging for my mouth?" He squeezes rough, sucking the tip and tugging on it with his teeth.

Electric sparks travel to my pussy, and I mewl.

"Tell me how much you want my cock between your legs."

"So fucking much." I rock my core against his lap. My pulse beats faster. I'm so close.

"Prove it. Keep rubbing that sweet cunt on my dick. Show me how fat you can make it. Soak my slacks."

He plunders my mouth, jerking my hips forward while I hump him. The friction from the sheer layers of fabric separating my panties from his pants sends a decadent thrill through me, and I explode.

Anson twists me off of him. My back lands on the plush comforter. He stands and drags my underwear down, splaying my legs when he's finished. I feel a trickle from my lower lips to my ass. He unbuttons his shirt and sheds his slacks and boxers, the heat of his gaze burning me the entire time.

And then with one thrust he's filling me.

"Oh, fu—" the words die on my lips, becoming incoherent mumbles of "more" and "harder."

I never enjoyed sex quite as much previous to Anson being in charge of my orgasms. And I initially thought his dirty mouth would get old, but nothing he says is degrading, so it hasn't. Sometimes I swear he saves the filthiest lines to tip me over the edge until he's taken me to the precipice and back so many times my pussy can't take it anymore and I'm clenching around him as he slams into me.

I grab his ass, meeting his every deep thrust.

"You want me to fill you everywhere, sweetheart?"

"Oh, please," I beg, slickness coating my thighs.

Anson's hand tucks between my butt and the hotel bed covers we are soiling. I feel his finger prod my slick asshole, and I see the devilish gleam stretch over his face.

I lift my hand. "Lick," I say, shoving two fingers into his mouth as he breaches my hole. My pussy clenches at the invasion, and I moan at the intense fullness even a single knuckle brings.

I'd refused to let anyone anywhere near my ass before him, and agreeing wasn't without negations. I was shocked he'd agree to any sort of ass play, let alone like it. But I love the power of commanding his orgasms, too.

Falling off the edge, my limbs are like jelly. It's a wonder I have the strength to move my arm to circle the pads of my fingertips in the same place on him.

"God, you're a demon." Anson bucks, coming with a roar, and collapsing on top of me.

He pants in sharp, hot breaths against my neck. Then disengages, dragging my limp body off the bed. I feel his cum dripping down my thighs.

"Let's get you cleaned up," he says.

My legs are rubbery as we make our way toward the bathroom. It is as opulent as the rest of the suite: marble sink and floor, plush towels, tiny bottles of designer soap and lotions.

Anson turns the glass-encased shower on to warm. The water cascades out of a rainfall showerhead. When the water temperature meets his expectations, he hits me with a devilish grin, and I know what's coming next. Me.

Neither of us wants kids. It took me years to gain control over my abilities. I was teased and a loner growing up. I can't see passing on my talents to an unsuspecting child. And because my mediumship has given me long-term health problems, I take care of birth control. But unlike a man with a breeding kink who fingers their cum back into a pussy before it drips out, Anson takes his own unique approach to making sure I don't get pregnant.

He moves me into the steamy shower, presses me against the tile, sinks to his knees, and lifts my leg over his shoulder.

Chapter Five

Anson

The next morning, I wrap a plush spa towel around my waist. Stepping out of the steamy bathroom, I grab another one from the towel rack, using it to rub the wetness from my short brown hair and wipe the drips from the St. Rita medal I wear around my neck.

The glass paneled doors to the Juliet balcony are wide open. Rae Lee is leaning on the railing, enjoying the street view as much as I'm enjoying mine. Her long white robe is cinched at her waist. Bent over, it accentuates her heart-shaped bottom. She's crossed her legs, and the soles of her feet peek from underneath the terry cloth.

She turns, popping the last morsel of a flaky croissant room service delivered before I showered into her mouth. Her back to the city, she stretches her arms over the railing. Her eyes rove over the water droplets, dripping from my neck down my bare chest.

I can't tell if the *mm-ing* sound is a compliment to the chef or approval of the hours I put in at the gym.

"Like what you see?" I tease.

"All of it. The hotel. The sights below." Her lips twist, using double entendre as her gaze falls beneath my navel.

I shoot her a wide grin, grabbing my clothes from the suitcase and sitting on the edge of the bed.

Rae Lee walks back into the suite, stopping at the room service cart to heat up my coffee from the carafe. My cup in one hand and fresh-squeezed orange juice in the other, she approaches me.

I take the refill, lift the cup to clink with her glass, and salute her. After taking a sip, she places her juice on the nightstand. Then she lifts the bottom of her plush robe and crawls onto the bed. I do the same on my side and shimmy back to the headboard, stretching out. Rae Lee snuggles into my chest and our bare legs intertwine.

"Thank you for bringing me here. I feel so spoiled." She places her palm over my heart.

"Everyone should be spoiled every so often." I kiss her temple. "There's nothing I wouldn't do for you, Raleigh."

I want Rae Lee to forget life's little troubles. I want to create lasting memories with her while we're here.

Regrettably, I can't protect my girlfriend from being a ghost magnet. That's why I wasn't sure bringing her to a city with a rich history was a good idea. Between the Civil War, Reconstruction, and The Great Fire, Charleston's seen its fair share of untimely deaths.

Discounting malevolent spirits, there's gotta be a lot of people reaching out from beyond the grave, trying to find peace or make amends.

We spend another half hour touching and talking. As much as I'd love to lie in bed all day making love to Rae Lee, we can do that at home. Eventually, we get dressed and make our way downstairs.

I stop to speak with the concierge as we exit the hotel, ensuring our dinner reservation stands.

"Is there anything we shouldn't miss?" I ask the lady manning the desk.

"There's always a haunted tour?" She offers me a pamphlet.

Beside me, Rae Lee adjusts the spaghetti strap of her sundress. She bites her lip, giving an almost imperceptible shake of her head.

"Yeah, we're good. Thanks, though."

Outside on the street, her anxiety doesn't diminish.

"What happened?" I nudge, reminding her she can talk to me without fear of judgment.

"The former hotel manager was there. I think Bernard died on duty because he had his name tag and uniform on. He had plenty of advice for the woman at the concierge desk staff about how to improve her performance, so it was 'spot-on'. Funny enough, Bernard didn't think we'd enjoy the ghost tour, either."

"Let me guess, when Bernard noticed you, he wanted us to say put so he could monopolize your time?"

"Yes. He thought I'd be a good conduit to bark

orders at everyone. I couldn't wait to get out of there."

"I'm sorry. I wish this were a real vacation for you."

"Anson, you could put me on a cruise ship in the middle of the ocean, and someone's dead relative, who decided to tag along, would stand there snapping their fingers and trying to get my attention. They all want my help with their unfinished business. What kills me is how loud the hotel manager was with his recriminations, and his criticisms were so... insignificant? It makes failing Agent Reed cut deeper."

I step in front of Rae Lee, grabbing her by the arms.

"You didn't fail Moira. You've explained to me before that spirits and residual energy are unpredictable. Maybe the victim only shows themselves at a certain time of day, and we were at the boat launch at the wrong time. Maybe they weren't there at all, and Moira didn't have you looking in the correct location. You can't blame yourself when the lead investigator is already grasping at straws."

I pause, regretting the way I treated my girlfriend when we met. I discounted her experiences because they were different from mine. I might've apologized to Rae Lee. Yet the consequences of my hostility, and my underestimation of her, add to the lingering self-doubt she has. I'll do anything to make my bad behavior up to her because I wish I'd never discounted someone who I've grown to respect. A woman I'll love for the rest of my life... and perhaps beyond.

Rae Lee isn't a grifter out to make a fat buck off somebody who is grieving. She isn't performing a magic act as part of a circus sideshow. My girlfriend receives a nominal fee for her services, which she donates because it makes her happy. However, right now whatever ISB is paying her doesn't seem like enough. I feel horrible that I've put her in a position where she feels guilty.

The one thing I know more than how much I love her is if Rae Lee didn't care so much about getting people the closure they deserve, she would shake off any perceived failure and spend the weekend pretending we drove from Brighton to Charleston without stopping.

Rae Lee plays with the rolled cuff of my lightweight button-up sleeve, fighting tears. So, I say exactly what I hope will help her achieve her own sense of peace.

"Would swinging by the site on the way home set your mind at ease?"

"Putting aside that you're assistant coaching Grant's baseball game, and we need to be there on time in order to cheer him on, I still don't think so." She sniffles. "I mean, what if you're right, and the victim is only there in the morning or late at night? Without Agent Reed giving me more to go on—and she didn't reveal to me if the person she's searching for is a man or woman, or anything else about them— we could be passing through when I'd still turn up with nothing."

I see her point. I was cautious about what I told her about the Tatton case. But we met at the little girl's home, and Pearl's mother was there. Rae Lee has zero information connecting Xavier Martin to the location. Flying entirely blind has her doubting the purpose for her abilities. Rae Lee wasn't put on this earth so a disgruntled former boss can yell at hotel employees about bad job performance.

"How about this? I'll call Agent Reed on Monday. We'll work out whatever details she's comfortable with you knowing that won't also cause concern that you've developed bias. Sound good?"

"Yes." Rae Lee agrees.

"Great. Now, let's see the sights."

We weave along the cobblestone streets from King Street to the French Quarter, jutting toward Waterfront park. Whenever an item in a window piques Rae Lee's interest, she pops in and out of a boutique. We pass museums and head toward the pier and Rainbow Row, circling back around after lunch to everything we missed.

Late in the afternoon, we return to the hotel to change for the evening. On the desk, where the strawberries were last night, there's sweet and savory petit fours underneath the cloche, and a bottle of champagne chilling in an ice bucket.

"There's an hour before our reservation. Let's save these for dessert." Rae Lee suggests.

Popping the cork on the champagne is premature, so "why not?" I agree.

"Be careful," she tells me. "I might get used to this pampering."

I wink.

Rae Lee grabs her clothes to go into the bathroom to get changed. Layla, who works at Paisley's Boutique, convinced her to splurge on a new dress for the trip. The white-and-black pinstripe fabric is tailored to her waist. It has a tall collar and a plunging neckline. She looks both casual and glamorous, pairing it with black heels. By some miracle, she's also twisted her short hair into a French knot. For the number of times I heard a *plink* on the bathroom floor, and Rae Lee's pained swearing, like someone was shooting a nail gun at her scalp, I'm surmising bobby pins.

Around her neck, dangling between her breasts and creating the illusion her perfect handful is ample cleavage,—god, it's fucking sexy as hell—is the vibrant orange sunstone necklace she prefers to wear from her collection.

"You're stunning," I tell her, slipping on my black sport coat.

Rae Lee saunters over, adjusting my lapels.

"You don't clean up so bad yourself, detective." She slides her palm behind my neck and pulls my lips toward hers.

Our tongues meet, and it's all I can do to not ruin her lipstick, peel the dress off of her, and say "fuck it" if we miss our reservation. But tonight is no ordinary night.

I clear my throat, trying to get a handle on the emerging problem in my pants. My dick's got a mind of its own, and it is about to ruin the plotting and scheming I did to get us here and convince Rae Lee we were celebrating our first anniversary.

Seated at the intimate restaurant, tucked into the historic block, the server pours red wine into our long-stemmed glasses. I order prime rib and Rae Lee decides on yellowfin tuna. It's the second time today she's ordered seafood, and the second time she's lifted her fork when she notices me eyeing her meal.

"You should have gotten the fish." She dabs a napkin at the corner of her mouth.

"Why, when I could have the best of both worlds?" I smirk, stabbing a satisfying bite of tuna from her plate.

When we finish the meal, I sign the receipt and grab her hand, guiding her to the exit. Outside, a private carriage awaits. Rae Lee asks the driver if she can pet the horse's muzzle. I stand with my hands in my pockets, watching my girlfriend baby-talk to the gentle animal. The carriage driver's in no hurry.

A few minutes later, she finishes and says, "All set. Let's go."

"Okay, get in." I motion to the carriage, here to take us back to the hotel.

"Anson! You shouldn't have done this!" she squeals.

"I wanted you to have a night to remember."

"It's been a vacation to remember. Promise me no more surprises after this."

"We're headed home tomorrow, so this'll be the last one." I shrug.

"Can we take this by the Pineapple fountain at the Waterfront Park?"

"Wherever you want to go." I prepaid the fare and planned to stop somewhere along the way.

The driver stops the carriage close to the fountain and asks, "Want to get out, miss? See it in the moonlight?"

"I think we do," I answer for Rae Lee.

We weave between the other tourists for a better look. A kid tosses a coin in and runs off. The wind blows. While she's distracted, brushing that lock of hair off her forehead, I step behind her.

Chapter Six

Rae Lee

The breeze blows off of the harbor, pushing the unruly lock of hair that won't ever stay in place into my eyes.

Really, for all the trouble it causes me, I should find a new hairstyle, but short is easy during the summer when it's humid. Plus, when it stays put, I love how sassy this cut is.

I hug myself and sigh contentedly, breathing in the ocean air, and tickled pink by the beauty of the fountain as the sun sets. The lights refract off the water, pouring from the curled pineapple stem down to the diamond shapes, and lapping against the sides. The teeming water is like white noise, eliminating all other sounds, relaxing me the way a weekend getaway should.

There are some moments I'd like to get trapped in. This is one, erasing all of my cares, is one of them.

"I think we should come back here someday," I say to Anson.

"I do, too." His voice comes from behind.

When he doesn't wrap his arms around me like I expect, I twist. That's when I realize all of the activity around the fountain has stopped. The spirit energy that's followed me around all day has disappeared. The other tourists hide themselves near the palm trees, quietly watching us. When I see Anson down on one knee, the sound of the fountain dissipates into the background, and all I hear is him.

"Maybe ten or even fifty years from now?" he asks, making my heart race.

Between his outstretched fingers he holds a thick platinum band.

"Raleigh, it sounds cliché to say I was a skeptic turned believer. And when you turned me, you turned me. Heart and soul. This year with you has taught me life isn't always what it seems. That I have to have the courage to look beyond what's in front of my face. Above all, you've taught me to see the world from a new perspective. That's made me not only a better cop, but a better man. Except, if I look any further for the person I want to spend the rest of my life with, what I'll miss out on is you. Be my wife."

I hold my shaking hand forward, and he slides the ring on. An emerald cut perches horizontally with two tapered diamonds on either side. I adore the bezel setting. It's unlikely to snag on anything.

But moreover, this ring is exactly what I'd have chosen. So, I know Anson's been listening to me ramble while I sit at the kitchen table, working on jewelry designs. In my experience, the most loving thing a person can do is listen.

"Yes. Yes, I'll absolutely marry you," I reply, tearing up.

He rises, crushing me to his chest, and spinning me around.

"I love you so much, Rae Lee," he says, kissing me when my feet touch the ground.

There's gentle clapping all around us, a shrill whistle, and congratulatory shouts as the crowd that gathered moves along with their evening.

I tuck my nose, admiring the ring and hiding my blush. "This is so beautiful, Anson. Thank you so much. I can't believe you did this in front of so many people."

He tips my chin. "I wanted you from the moment I saw you, Raleigh. But I want everyone to know I'm proud that Rae Lee Chatham chose me forever."

"For eternity." I one-up him, cupping his stubbled cheeks, and holding his forehead to mine.

"You better believe it, or I'm the next person haunting you."

I laugh, hugging him tightly. "I love you."

"Obviously, Layla," I say when Anson asks me if I want a maid of honor.

From the moment we buckled in this morning to return home in time for Grant's baseball game, we've been discussing what kind of wedding we want. We're leaning toward another nice vacation on the heels of a no-frills ceremony. It's a matter of when, since we left the hotel hours ago, and back-to-back trips feel decadent. We'll deal with *where* to go when we have the timing squared away.

"Which means we need to include Julian, which is fine." Anson adds Layla's better half to the guest list.

Because we live in Layla & Julian's house, Anson and he get along well.

"And Chaim?" He's not only Anson's boss, but his closest friend. "Plus, his wife. It only makes sense if he's standing up for you. What about your sisters, your parents, my parents, Delores, and Grant? Do you think they'll feel left out?" I shift in my seat, crossing my legs.

"Is this wedding getting bigger than we bargained for? You said you were more comfortable with small. Intimate. You know, it can just be us and the Justice of the Peace?"

"I'd like someone there to share the memory with."

"Well, I'll be there."

"I should hope so!" I grab his knee. "We could just elope?"

Anson shrugs.

He went out of his way this weekend to make the proposal special. It's his wedding too. I can't make this everything about me. I know his question about Layla was leading. He wants to include his family somehow, but without the extravagance and back-breaking cost of his sisters' church weddings, when we can put the money to better use on a honeymoon or a new home.

"Aren't you the same woman who is worried someone will feel left out? How about the six of us at City Hall, and then supper with family and whomever else we'd like to invite?" Anson suggests the private function room at Mark-39.

"Oh, I like that idea! Then we can bypass the dry chicken or rubbery beef, and everyone can order what they'd like to eat."

"So, it's settled. When are you asking Layla?"

"Is as soon as we get home too soon?" I fidget in my seat again.

"Excited?" Anson asks.

"Yes. But we've also been on the road a long time. I need to use the restroom." I chuckle. "Do you think we can pull over?"

"That gas station we stopped at on the way down is around the bend."

"Thank goodness, and thank you." I let out a relieved breath.

This time, Anson waits in the car at the service station. I offer to get him coffee. There are a few houses tucked nearby, but for the most part we're in the middle of cornfields.

Based on how clean the store looks, I'm sure the owner does good business. However, most convenience stores have a policy that restrooms are for paying customers. I won't be the person who skips out on buying something.

The woman I met in the parking lot notices me as I get out of the car. She hustles, approaching me. Needing to relieve my bulging bladder, I *really* can't stop to talk to her right now. On top of that, I've concentrated so hard on keeping spirits out today. Even the dead hotel manager, when he pestered the concierge to congratulate Anson and me.

I'm relaxed from the trip, and the happiest I can remember being. Aren't I allowed to float in the joy bubble over getting engaged for a little while longer? My fiancé's not wrapped up, thinking about the cases waiting on his desk at work. Just because dead people talk to me doesn't seem like a legitimate reason why my feet have to hit the ground running before Monday.

I dart past the huddled man and into the store, thrilled—yes, thrilled!—the restroom sign is clearly marked.

After I take care of business and wash my hands, I stop and doctor a coffee for Anson. The brew in a paper cup will cool off fast, so I forgo the bottled water. I don't want a drink because stopping again means it will take longer to get home and share our good news with friends.

The pregnant girl behind the register rings me up. Her name tag reads Amara. As she counts out the change, I can't help thinking she's as pretty as Layla, and wondering if she's having a boy or a girl. I think a girl would grow up to look just like her.

I slide the extra cash I have from breaking a larger

bill at the Charleston City Market across the counter. Behind me, the door chimes and someone walks in whom the clerk pays attention to.

"I'm almost finished, Sidney." Amara says to a man about her age who slips behind the register.

Sidney kisses the top of her head, and I get a wash of emotion from the two of them. I sense he cares deeply for her and for her baby. Despite being in this together, her love for him isn't romantic.

I hold my palm up to accept the coins and receipt.

She reaches out, and I glimpse a thin red line of interconnected hearts tattooed above her hand. The chain is unbroken. One upside down, one right side up, the hearts encircle her wrist like a bracelet.

Her fingertips graze my skin. As soon as we touch, a sweat breaks out under my nose. My entire body jolts.

Blinking, I try to shake the vision away.

"I hope it's a girl," I say.

No, don't do this, please! I think.

My knees go weak as my eyes land on the terrified woman behind the counter. Spots dot my vision, and I'm falling away from her. Down, down, down until I'm dragged under.

Chapter Seven

Xavier

...I'd know Amara's knock anywhere. She has the camper door open and is sitting on the bed that's hardly big enough to fit me before I tell her to come in.

"I'm sorry I'm late," she says, out of breath and blowing on her hands to warm them up.

It's dark outside, and she's run all the way from her dad's house near the gas station to the woods where I've parked my tow-behind.

"I'm glad you could come at all." I lift the pink tulip-print sleeping bag she stole from the linen closet, and she tucks into my side.

It doesn't make a difference that it's off-season and the campground is closed. I don't have an electric hookup for a space heater anyway. The only way to stay warm is sharing body heat under a pile of blankets.

"Oh, are you hungry?" Amara rifles through her coat pocket, producing two shriveled hot dogs in a zip-top bag. "Sorry, I shut off the roller grill early, but they still dried out. Tomorrow I'll see if the sandwich delivery guy brings any garden salads, and I'll hide one at the back of the case until it reaches the sell-by date."

The nights she closes, Amara brings me whatever expired snacks are left that need tossing. The nights I close, everything makes it into the garbage. I won't let Mr. Henderson accuse me of stealing or dock my pay for an overpriced wiener.

I've worked at the gas station for a few months. Her dad's a fucking hard-ass. The kind of prick who tells me to show up at nine, then changes the schedule to nine-thirty, knowing I don't got a phone. Then he waits a half hour to say I'm early and refuses to pay me for taking out the garbage or making sure the coffee is fresh for his regular customers.

According to Mr. Henderson, I can't stock a shelf to save my life. I swear he's even pissed on the floor to make me go back and clean the restroom a second time. Outside of being brilliant at science, nothing Amara does is right either. I'm not sure how Amara's mother put up with the guy.

At least, I get to see Amara. At work, and after her dad pops the sleeping pills he started taking after her mom died. He'd probably shit a brick if he found out she sneaks out to see me. It was important to Amara's mom for her to be the first in her family to go to college. I'm definitely not moving up in the world, living in a shitty camper with no electricity, and eating expired food.

I put the overcooked protein on a ledge. "Beggars can't be choosers. You probably shouldn't be here if you don't want your dad to catch you before prom. He'll ground you forever."

And I'll lose the only person worth sticking around for.

"Meh, it's not like I really want to go with Sidney or he wants to go with me, either. He's got a massive crush on the guy who sits in front of him in calculus. Maybe I'll come hang out with you instead."

"Why would you ditch your junior prom to hang out with a friend?"

"The question you should be asking is why would I sneak out and steal shitty hot dogs so you didn't starve if all I wanted was your friendship, Xavier?" Amara presses her lips to mine.

I know getting involved with me is the wrong move for her. But I kiss her back.

Amara's future's been mapped out forever. There are eight months before she begins her freshman year.

I'm no dummy. However, her grades, compared to what mine were in high school, make me look like an illiterate fool. I couldn't afford college even if I wanted to go, but I'm excited for her and proud of her for getting into a great school.

I glance over the top of her early acceptance letter. My smile falls, seeing her frown.

"What's wrong?" I reach over, brushing her hair behind her shoulder. "Babe, you're not worried I won't come through for you, are you? You're not getting rid of me that easy. I'll camp in your dorm parking lot if I have to."

I'm in love with Amara. Before she even applied, we'd talked about how she'll only be an hour away in the fall. Amara's dad will make her work at the gas station over the holidays. We'll see one another all the time. Not to mention, with her gone, I can pick up her shifts and save extra money to support us later on.

"It's not that." Amara twists her hands, looking everywhere but at me.

"Then what is it?"

"I don't want to go."

"Babe, you have to go to college." It's her ticket out of here and out from under her controlling father's thumb.

"I want to go to college. I just don't want to go to college near Charlotte. I want to go to Pinewood State."

"Why don't you apply there?" It's where I thought I wanted to go, and the idea of Amara attending Pinewood excites me.

"Because it's not what they wanted." Meaning her mom and dad. "My mom planted this dream in my dad's head that I should go to this school because its campus is beautiful and where she'd have gone had she had the chance."

Family dynamics are hard for me to understand. I never met my dad. Quitting soccer and caring for my mom before she died was the most time I spent with her. Until then, I was clueless about how hard she worked to afford the next size up in cleats and keep a roof over our heads. Any money I thought I'd get went toward paying her medical bills.

I was already eighteen when Mom passed. The rest of my senior year, I pulled all-night shifts at a factory to feed myself and went to school during the day. The principal handed me my diploma and the landlord an eviction notice within hours of each other.

When I asked where I was supposed to go, the landlord let me buy the camper he was about to list on a buy-sell-trade site. Then, my phone drained and my alarm didn't go off one too many times. That was the beginning of the end of a decent paying job that let me save a few bucks. After that, the factory manager got nit-picky about everything from my appearance to the two spots I took up with my tow-behind in the parking lot. They didn't care that I was homeless and trying to get back on my feet.

Knowing what I know now—moving on and dealing with Amara's hard ass dad as a boss—I probably could've parked the trailer illegally. But hindsight is 20/20, and I was just a kid with nobody looking out for him, who got frustrated, shot off his mouth, and got fired.

"It's not even a bad college!" Amara throws up her

arms. "Sidney wants to go there. I should just suck it up."

"No, you shouldn't. Follow your own dreams. Apply to Pinewood. See what happens."

"With what money, Xavier? My dad said by paying me to work for him, he was already paying the fee for this application." She shakes the paper.

That's so unfair. It's also consistent with the way he treats women. Amara's mother died in the parking lot of a ruptured appendix. He told his wife the pain was all in her head. The very next day, he expected Amara to step into her mother's shoes, both at home and at the convenience store.

"Your dad's also depending on you to get scholarships and take out loans. So, if you're paying for college on your own, shouldn't you have a say in where you go?" I sit forward and pull out my wallet.

I have a hundred-dollar bill I found cleaning out my mother's drawers. It was in a graduation card addressed to me, which makes me feel like my mom was aware she wasn't going to make it for a lot longer than she let on. Even falling on hard times, I've kept it for sentimental reasons.

"I want you to have this," I say.

"But—"

—but nothing, Amara. I'm never amounting to anything. At least let me die having paid it forward."

"Don't be melodramatic."

"Don't roll over, baby." I pause, regretting for a moment I'm about to use the shitty circumstances we bonded over against her. "I bet if your mom had to do it all over again, she'd be on your side, too."

The air is warm. Well, warmer than it's been all winter. Amara and I won't have to huddle under the blankets in the camper much longer. *Not that we haven't found ways to stay warm.* Springtime is coming. After August, we won't have to look over our shoulders whenever we're on a walk in the woods, and hear a twig snap.

To celebrate her acceptance to Pinewood—and the fact that neither of us can see our breath in front of our faces—we've ventured out. They're doing bridge work a mile from the brush I'm squatting in on national forest land. We're not afraid anyone will see us and report back to her father because the road crew closed the road in either direction.

Stars dance in the night sky. The bridge, bathed in moonlight, is about as romantic as I can afford. Although things are looking up. There's a possibility someday I can give Amara everything she deserves.

"I've got a surprise for you." Unable to remember the last time I felt this happy, I lift a leg over the parapet and straddle the concrete. My toes dangle a foot off the road on one side, and *a lot* more than a foot down on the other.

"Ooh, I love surprises." Amara pushes up her sleeve, exposing the gold bracelet I gave her that was my mother's.

Although I think Mom got it from someone other than my DNA donor, I heard her once say it was a gift from her first love. That stuck with me, and I wanted Amara to have it.

"What is it?" she asks, giving me a playful peck on the lips.

"A friend I played soccer with has an off-campus apartment at Pinewood State. They're looking for a roommate. I said I was interested."

"I can't believe you're going to move with me!" Amara squeals.

When she hugs me, my thighs tighten like I'm riding a horse to stay balanced.

"How hard can it be to find a job at a gas station?" I shrug when she lets go. "If I can save a few bucks, I thought I'd try taking a community college class or two. Maybe I could be a licensed plumber or do HVAC or something."

I love Amara. I want to be the best version of myself for her. But most of all, I don't want her trapped like her mom was by some guy who's turned into her dad.

Lately, he's been at home asleep more than he's minding his business. I suppose that's been good for us. Amara hasn't even told him yet that she's going to Pinewood and studying horticulture and agroecology instead of engineering, which is what her mom pushed on Amara as a major.

The more heart-to-hearts Amara and I have had since we started seeing each other over a year ago, the more I'm convinced her mom wasn't a bad person. I think her lack of opportunity got her stuck in a lousy situation. She put pressure on Amara to get good grades and to go to college so her daughter could escape a life she couldn't.

Maybe that's why my mom worked so hard to pay for me to play soccer, even though it hurt that she missed more games than she attended.

"Whatever you decide to do, you'll be brilliant." She voices her confidence in me.

I flip my dangling leg roadside to hold her.

"I wanna build a life with you, Amara. I want you to be as proud of me as I am of you."

"What? I am proud of you, silly." She tucks herself into my chest, and I wrap my arms around her. "You never know why bad things happen to good people. You didn't do anything wrong to deserve what happened to you, Xavier. Maybe if my mom was here for me to talk to and your mom was around when you graduated, you could have gotten a soccer scholarship and we would have met at Pinewood." She burrows into my chest. "I love you, so, so much. Things were different when my mom was alive. Being stuck here with my dad felt like my soul was ripped in two, and when you came into my life, it was like you sewed it back together and filled the empty places she left behind."

She looks up at me, a beacon in the darkness. I've often wondered why I took the shitty-ass job and why my boss's daughter would risk stealing food for me, but now I know. It's because we were meant to be together.

Right before I kiss Amara, I see nothing but love shining in her eyes.

"Oh," she gasps as we pull apart.

The tiny hearts on her bracelet have gotten caught in the threads of my sweater. She tugs. I grab her wrist to stop her. I can get it untangled if she'll hold still.

The quick motion unbalances me. I'm tumbling backward.

The expression on Amara's face changes from adoration to terror. She reaches out, but it's too late.

My arms and legs pinwheel. I hear the whoosh of air by my ears. My spine hits the water with a terrible sting, and the cold makes me gasp. My lungs fill, and I choke on brackish water. Something hard hits my head, erasing my sluggish thoughts of swimming to the surface.

Chapter Eight

Anson

Through the convenience store window, I watch Rae Lee approach the counter. Knowing she'll be out momentarily, I get distracted searching Mark-39's website on my phone.

Wedding planning is going smoothly. Rae can't abide a fuss. So, I'm not surprised at her suggestion to have a single important person for each of us there when we exchange vows. I also like the idea of our friends and family gathering at the restaurant after we say "I do." Mark-39 is where I consider our first date happened.

The hair on the back of my neck prickles. I look up from scrolling the restaurant menu, and Rae Lee's gone.

Getting out of the car, I hustle into the service station with the sinking sensation she shouldn't have gone in there alone. The glass door hits something solid, but I squeeze inside.

My heart comes to a screeching halt. My mouth is so dry, I can't swallow.

Rae Lee is unconscious in front of the counter. Brown liquid soaks the side of her light blue t-shirt and khaki linen shorts. The coffee paper cup and the darker lid have rolled away separately. Coins litter the floor. The register is open with dollar bills scattered over the till.

"Oh my God, wake up, Amara! Help! Somebody do something!" The young man I saw walking in a few minutes ago is squatting behind the register, holding onto the young girl who was working here last week.

His external freak-out mirrors my internal one.

"What the hell happened?" I yell to get his attention.

I hit my knees and the emergency button on my cell phone in unison.

"I don't know. She just passed out." His only concern is the pregnant clerk. I don't even think he realizes anyone else collapsed.

Certain speakerphone is on, I let my phone clatter to the floor. I try to rouse my fiancé, careful not to move her in case she's injured.

"Rae Lee, Rae—Raleigh?"

I rub a hand over her hair. Blood covers it. My pulse speeds up. The instinct to protect someone I love wars with my training. I have to stop myself from dragging her lax body off the shitty waxed tiles and cradling her in my lap.

"911. What's your emergency?" The operator

comes on the line.

"This is Detective Anson Ames." I begin by identifying myself and the location of the gas station. "Two women have collapsed inside the store. One has a head injury. The other is pregnant."

"I'm alerting the local authorities, Detective Ames. Are you able to stay on the line until the units arrive?"

"Yes," I bark, unintentionally.

Adrenaline courses through my veins.

"Are you safe where you are, detective? Do you smell gas?" they ask.

I sniff the air. "No. I'm inside with one more person, so I don't think it is carbon monoxide."

The guy holding the pregnant clerk has been in here long enough that any odorless leak causing the women to collapse should have affected him, too.

I don't get it. Nothing about the scene makes sense.

"Please don't move anyone unless you have to," the operator says.

Sirens fill the air, coming from the volunteer fire department we drove past a mile or so back. A firetruck with an ambulance on its heels turns into the parking lot. The crews are inside, assessing the situation, when a police cruiser circumvents another driver, pulling around the pumps.

"Everyone's here." I end the call with the 911 operator, easing out of the way for the paramedics to get to Rae Lee.

An EMT flashes a penlight in Amara's eyes. Like she hadn't wanted to awaken from a nap, she groggily comes to.

Rae Lee's reactions are slower. She moans, trying to lift her arm to touch the bloody mess in her hair. A wince. She blanches. If her face could lose any more color, it has. The EMT grabs hold of her arm, crossing it over her chest.

I overhear the radio squawk, asking for a second ambulance to take them to the county hospital. The grumpy gas station owner storms out of the office, grousing about the commotion. He and the kid bicker.

"Figures you're more fucking concerned about whether a customer will sue you or if this stops Amara from showing up for work tomorrow than you are about your daughter or grandchild." The younger man tells the older to fuck off and not to bother showing up at the hospital.

When the paramedics load Rae Lee onto a stretcher and move her toward the ambulance, her eyelids finally flutter. She pulls in a deep breath. It doesn't match the barely audible sound slipping from her lips.

"Moira."

I knock lightly on the hospital room door in the maternity ward. When a male voice tells us to come in, I push it open, letting Agent Reed proceed first. Moira's dressed in uniform, whereas the light gray shorts and white polo I'm wearing are coffee-stained.

"Don't say anything," Sidney grunts under his breath to the young woman reclining in the bed.

The same girl who waited on me last week behind the counter at the gas station has the covers pulled up to her middle. One arm rests protectively over her protruding stomach. Sidney has his index finger linked with hers on the other hand. She snatches it away, wiping tears from her ruddy face.

"Amara Henderson?" Agent Reed pulls out her notepad. "We'd like to talk to you about the event that happened at your father's gas station earlier this afternoon."

"Now's not a good time," Sidney interjects. Amara tries to hush him, but he continues, focused on her well-being. "The doctor said."

"Any contractions I have are Braxton Hicks."

"It doesn't matter. You passed out when that other lady hit the ground, and I'm the one who caught you. Letting them question you when you should be resting is foolish."

The way Amara looks at Sidney, it's obvious she cares about him. But I doubt she loves him, and I didn't need either Amara or Rae Lee carried away by an ambulance to help me figure that out.

Amara lets go of Sidney's hand. "Is that woman okay?" she asks.

Moira turns to me to explain.

"Miss Chatham is resting downstairs," I say.

The doctor is keeping her overnight for observation. We won't be cheering on Grant's team this afternoon, and I'm not sure which of us blames themselves more. Rae Lee has a fractured elbow. She burned her hand from tightening her grip around the paper coffee cup and crushing it. The ER doctor placed six stitches in her scalp, and she has a concussion.

But in the ER—when she opened her eyes and painfully whispered, "Moira" for a second time—I was never happier to brush the swoop of hair that stuck out of the bandage covering her head, and follow her lead, contacting Agent Reed immediately.

Deep down, I knew Rae Lee had to have had pieces of the puzzle. Like Moira Reed, she just didn't have the one that fit them together and made them make sense.

Two of the three people Rae Lee encountered on our first pit stop at the gas station are connected to Amara. The woman was her mother, and Xavier Martin was the man huddled outside the door. Having seen my then-girlfriend communicate with Mrs. Henderson, Xavier took advantage of Rae Lee. Focused on the wedding and her own happiness, her guard was down, and he jumped her.

"Ask me how I feel about that." I dared Moira when she found out.

As a rookie cop, I got ambushed on patrol. I've never forgotten the experience. It molded me into who I am today. I suss out the cases Rae Lee consults. I'm strict about anything coming near her I think will come back to haunt her, let alone hurt her. That a fucking dead man attacked and took over the body of the love of my life? Right now, everyone should presume Rae Lee's consulting days are over.

I even hesitated leaving her alone in her hospital room.

While Amara Henderson isn't a flight risk, she is waiting for discharge papers. Agent Reed preferred questioning Amara before she and Sidney came up with another cover story.

"I'm curious how well you knew Xavier Martin, the man who worked for your father." Moira speaks after I explain Rae Lee will be fine.

"What does he have to do with that blonde lady passing out?" In for a dime, in for a dollar, Sidney slides his too-close chair closer to the bed.

"The lady is my fiancée. Special Agent Reed enlisted Rae Lee's help to solve the Martin case."

"Did you and Xavier often work the same shifts?" Moira asks.

"Yes," Amara says in an I've-told-you-this tone. She did when she mentioned Xavier lived in the teardrop camper to Agent Reed. Otherwise, Amara was tight-lipped with her overbearing father using his surveillance system to observe the interview.

"Were you friendly outside of work?"

"What difference does that make?" The man she's been passing off as the father of her child interrupts, grabbing back onto her hand.

"We were friends." Amara cuts Sidney off, shirking his hold.

"Any chance you were more than friends?"

Amara looks out the window at the horizon. "If I told you we were, are you willing to tell me what...

what she is?"

"What do you mean, Amara?" Agent Reed plays coy.

Amara's lip trembles. "I saw everything like a flash before Miss Chatham passed out. Every moment we spent together." She licks, then bites her lip. "I thought they were my memories. But they weren't. They were his…Xavier's. Because I also saw him kicking the soccer ball down the field before his mom died. She was in the stands, and he was…He was so fucking happy because she almost never showed up to a game. He was so good that he should have gotten a scholarship, did you know that?" She rubs her belly like a genie, talking more to her stomach than to us. "If she hadn't died, we wouldn't have met. I've been so lost without him. But he's been waiting outside the store for you to get here, grateful we still had a future." Amara glances up, all but ignoring everyone in the room but me. "Miss Chatham, she's one of those people, right? The ones who help people cross over?" Her questions sound like pleas.

"Miss Chatham has a way of connecting with those we've lost, yes," I respond.

"Did she help Xavier cross over?"

"I—I don't know. I don't think so."

"He can't be stuck there forever, Sid." Amara's face crumbles. She uses the butt of her palm to wipe her tears, and I notice the tattoo Rae Lee told Moira about earlier.

"Can I ask when you got that tattoo? Agent Reed mentioned you didn't have it when she first spoke with you."

The pattern of hearts is identical to the bracelet found tangled in the weave of Xavier Martin's sweater.

Amara swallows. "A month or so later."

"When you found out you were pregnant?"

The young girl nods.

"Xavier Martin is the father of your baby," I confirm.

Another head shake, though she glances at a crestfallen Sidney.

"You shouldn't have told them," he murmurs.

"You shouldn't have told my dad it was yours to get your parents to back off about why you never brought girls home. Now, none of us are going to Pinewood."

I use simple logic; two teenagers can't afford to have a baby their freshman year of college. Whatever Sidney's parents' beef is—and I'm not stupid. I can read between the lines—they're insisting he forgo his studies, step up, and care for the grandchild they think he fathered.

"Not going to college is better than going to jail," Sidney tells her.

"Amara, what happened to Xavier?" Agent Reed inquires.

"Xavier was sitting on the side of the bridge. It was one of the few secluded places we could go without anyone seeing us and telling my dad. We were talking about Xavier moving along with me when I was supposed to leave for Pinewood. We were just happy, planning our future one minute," her shoulders pop to her ears, and the smile of the memory playing on her lips fades. "The next minute, the bracelet he gave me got stuck. When we tried to get it loose, he fell. Everything happened so fast." She bites her lip, tears spilling from her eyes. "He disappeared backward over the edge. I looked for him. I really did. But it was so dark. So I ran to Sidney's, and he drove me back."

"We searched the riverbank...A long way...But the closer to daybreak it got, the foggier it was, and he was just...Gone," the kid adds, staring at the bedsheets.

"My dad was livid when he pulled back the curtain and saw Sidney had drove me home."

That makes it easy to use her best friend as a cover for the baby daddy.

"You never thought to call 911?" Although the coroner's report indicated it was unlikely Martin survived the fall, Moira tempers her annoyance.

Hardly.

She's been working this case for almost a year. She knows that despite the warm night, the water temperature was freezing. A human's first reaction to icy cold water is to gasp. That's what Xavier Martin did. Submerged in the river, his reflexes took over. He inhaled, and he drowned.

"Amara, stop talking. You need a lawyer." Sidney tries to silence her. She wants to argue until he covers her belly with his palm and says, "This baby already lost one parent. They can't afford to lose two."

Rae Lee

I wave my card over the payment terminal. It's about the easiest thing I can manage in the entire transaction. Designing jewelry with a broken elbow on my dominant side?

That's completely out of the question.

"Do you mind?" I point a dopey finger sticking out of the sling.

My favorite Baked Beans barista slides my sparkling lemon and blueberry iced tea over.

While the next customer orders, I stand to the side and put my credit card into my phone wallet. It takes one, two, three, tries to slip that into my back pocket. I have on drawstring shorts so I don't have to futz zipping or buttoning them, but a top that buttons because getting shirts over my head is a beast. I'm also wearing a ball cap with Grant's team logo on it to protect my stitches.

"By the time this heals, I'll be pro," I insist, speaking as much to them as giving myself a pep talk.

The customer behind me smiles. The barista waves, telling me to get well soon.

One week post-fall and I feel like soon can't come soon enough. I've had autoimmune flares since Anson and I got together. He's always taken great care of me. However, having to wait for Anson to cut my dinner into bite-size pieces *again* last night was humbling.

Cold beverage in hand—the fully functioning one— I exit and walk toward Paisley's bouquet to make a silly face at Layla, who is working today. In return, she stops folding shirts for a display and sticks out her tongue at me like the goofy emoji. Pressing my nose against the glass bops the baseball hat. I readjust it and proceed around the building and up a block to the fields.

Grant is playing a doubleheader this afternoon. Treating myself to Baked Beans was part of the first seventh-inning stretch of the day.

"How'd you make out?" His grandmother, Delores, sees me approaching the metal bleachers.

"Everything takes practice." *And twice as long to do.*

"I'm surprised Anson let you leave home. Your fall shook him up."

A look passes between us that tells me Delores hasn't seen Anson hover this way since her daughter, Grant's mother, died.

"Eh, he knew you'd be here to babysit me." I try to keep it light. "Thanks for trusting me to look both ways when I crossed the street."

Delores slaps her knee when she laughs. Immediately after, I hear the strike of a bat against a ball. She claps, yelling to Grant to stop the batter from stealing second.

I retake my seat on the hot bleachers, less surprised Angeline appears next to me now than she hadn't yet. Warmth tickles up my spine, and I look over at her.

That *is* abnormal. I go out of my way to limit our interactions.

Before her untimely death, Angeline and Anson dated. The first time she made herself known to me, I got the feeling Angeline was jealous. And maybe she was, but...

"You're happy for us," I say, out loud and amazed.

Angeline pretends to ignore me the way I've done to her. However, a secret smile plays on her lips; one I'm not sure is satisfaction at the throw Grant made from the outfield that got the opposing player out at second base or just what.

"I can live with happy," I murmur.

If she were a corporeal being, my shoulder would have nudged hers.

As the teams change sides, Delores spares me a glance. There's a uniqueness to our relationship. Anson is active in Grant's life. He's on the field now, coaching and being the best male influence a teenage boy can get. I'm the new girlfriend, um, fiancée.

Delores is also aware of my abilities and has never once asked me if Angeline makes her presence known or if I can pass on a message to her daughter. It's strange how something so simple can make a person feel appreciated for who they are, and not what they can do for someone else. The more weekends I've spent with Delores cheering on Grant, the more I feel like we're a unit.

I spot Layla at the corner of the bleachers. She uses a paper to shield her eyes from the sun, peering around. She spies me and pounds up the metal stairs, her long brown curls bouncing behind her.

"What are you doing here?" I ask.

"I'm on my break. Here." She takes the spot Angeline vanishes from and hands me a flat notecard.

"What's this?"

"An invite to your bachelorette party. We were going to kidnap you. But we figured you'd had enough surprises for a while."

"Aw! I didn't expect you to throw me a party when I asked you to be my maid of honor."

I throw my good arm around Layla. She squeezes me back.

"Ya didn't expect to pass out and break your elbow either. At least this is a fun not-surprise, since you decided to push the wedding date off until you don't have to bedazzle that sling."

My cheek pulls. I'm bummed Anson and I won't be getting married until I'm out of the splint and have started physical therapy. Though it's made coordinating the guest list and reception after our small nuptials less frantic. Plus, now I'm excited my bestie has done the unexpected and is throwing me a party.

"Thank you for this." I shake the invite.

Having been taken advantage of for my unusual talents, I used to be a massive introvert, happy with the crumbs of my best friend's attention. In all honesty, I didn't understand I was Layla's ride-or-die until she told me so. When Paisley invited me to an open house at the boutique—an event I thought I was supposed to be a vendor at—and Layla introduced me to the friend group she made when she and Julian moved to Brighton, that changed. I'm excited to see who shows up.

Layla pshes. "You said I didn't have to buy a horrible dress I'd only wear once, and that you didn't want a bridal shower. A night on the town is nothing. It makes me feel like I'm actually doing something for this wedding."

"You are!"

"Standing in a judge's chambers with a goofy smile plastered on my face while you get hitched is not my idea of coming through for you, Rae."

"You'll hold my bouquet when we exchange rings?" I offer.

Layla's brow pops. "Get serious."

"I am!" I insist.

"Please, I'm not doing anything you wouldn't do for me."

"Well, I love you and appreciate you for this." I tuck the notecard to my heart.

Clutching the door frame, I step on the heels of my shoes and slip them off. Then I toe them onto the shoe rack by the apartment door, which Anson brought over from his place when he followed me back to live in mine.

Greeting us at the doorway, Fred winds himself around my ankle, rubbing his kitty head against my calf.

"Watch yourself," Anson cautions, picking up the cat and depositing him on the bed. "The doctor said that recovering from your concussion could last up to fourteen days. I don't want a return visit to the hospital for a second set of stitches."

My fiancé's been overprotective since Xavier jumped me. I can't say I blame him. Except, seven days with my phone and the TV remote in Anson's custody because "screen time is bad for head injuries" makes for a dull recovery. Before Grant's doubleheader, the walls of our studio apartment were closing in on me. The splint and sling gave me a wonky sunburn, but I'm glad I got out for an entire day.

I growl, frustrated at the rules he makes, supposedly for my own good. I'm not used to anyone taking care of me the way he does when he is home. My parents love me, but they were a bit less hover-y?

Not that I broke any bones or had a ghost take over my body when I was a kid.

"Now what do we do?" I ask, knowing full-well Anson's bushed after coaching two baseball games, and tomorrow he's back on duty.

"I am taking a shower," he replies, tugging his sweaty, dusty t-shirt off to reveal his broad chest. He unbuttons his jeans. I catch a hint of the color of his boxers. Seeing my interest, he doesn't unzip his pants the rest of the way.

My lower lip juts out, and I receive a head shake and a huff under his breath in response.

Butt covered, Anson disappears into the bathroom. He shuts the door, stopping me from peeking, and I hear the water in the clawfoot tub turn on and the metal rings scrape against the rod as Anson draws the wraparound shower curtain around the tub.

Every time I've tried to get Anson in the mood, he's shut me down. I suggested putting a pillow at the headboard so that if any amorous activities got rough, I didn't bonk my head. Even that was a no-go. The last time he and I had sex was on vacation. If this drought keeps up, by next weekend I'll need to grease the drawer pulls on my nightstand for the number of times I will have opened it to find a toy to play with while he's at work.

No jewelry making. No phone or TV. No orgasms. Too much time to ponder my regrets.

Getting well soon blows.

Not even my cat, who bolted underneath the bed frame where he prefers to hide, wants to keep me company.

Perhaps leaving home today wasn't such a good idea. I normally like my independence and the time to myself to create, but the thought of being alone after a slice of the outside world depresses me. At this point, given how Angeline acted at the ball field, I'd even accept her company. And it was Angeline hovering over me at Anson's place, until I couldn't take it anymore, that made me move back in at Layla and Julian's.

Since he's not around to command me not to, I tidy up our cozy space, finding my stupid blackout mask underneath the hospital discharge papers on the table.

I harrumph, walk the few paces to the bed, and flop my ass down, running the binding trimming the black silk through my fingers.

Working the occasional case with Anson makes me feel closer to him and like my abilities are useful and the universe had a purpose for creating me with oddities others find it hard to understand. Wearing the mask wasn't entirely useless, but it wasn't as useful as I'd wished.

The shower turns off. Steam escapes the bathroom as Anson opens the door. My fiancé clutches a towel to his waist, aiming for the dresser with his clothes in it. Water drips onto the floor from his hair. His hurried actions are nothing like the lazy saunter he did, walking around the luxurious hotel room with the bath sheet wrapped around his waist and droplets covering his lickable chest.

It's like Anson's ashamed of me seeing him naked.

"Whatcha got?" He veers over, approaching me.

I snap the elastic. Then lift the mask, twirling it around my index finger to show him.

"I know what I experienced helped Moira solve her case, except I wonder what my impressions would have been if I hadn't worn this silly thing," I admit.

I feel like I should have known Xavier was the cold man waiting outside the convenience store door, and connected Amara's mother to her sooner. Sensed something that linked Amara to the case sooner.

Anson sits on the bed and takes the mask from me. "Don't discount the effectiveness of a technique before you've had opportunities to hone your skills. Maybe you need more practice?"

He removes my ball cap and covers my eyes with the silky mask. Tugging me to stand, his towel brushes the front of my legs and drops, covering my feet. Unable to see, my pulse beats wildly. I want to ask Anson what he's doing, but I don't want him to stop.

The fasteners on my sling make a ripping sound. As the neck loosens, he gently removes it. I cradle my elbow to my side. He un-tucks my blouse, unbuttoning it and cautiously pulling the short sleeves over my arms. His dexterous fingers make quick work of my bra clasp. My breasts tumble out. I can tell how far away he is by the heat radiating off his body.

His fingers slip under my waistband, and he draws the shorts over my hips.

"Did you have a sinister plan in mind when you forgot to put on panties, Raleigh?" His playful voice portrays the beaming expression on his face.

I press my tongue to the cupid's bow of my lip.

"Guilty as charged."

His knuckle runs over my belly, dipping at my navel, and tracing the cleft of my pussy. Heat pools between my legs, and sparks light up my skin.

Two fingers separate my folds, skirting my slick clit and making me hyperaware. He thrusts them inside me and I gasp, lifting to my tip-toes. Reaching for his shoulder to anchor myself, Anson is lowering to kneel. With his hand keeping a steady rhythm, he presses his nose to my mound. I hear a satisfied inhale before he lifts my leg over his shoulder. Then his fingertips dig into my ass cheek, holding me balanced to his face. His warm tongue darts out, licking my center, swirling around my sensitive clit, and then sucking it into his mouth.

This time when I fall, I fall into bliss.

Epilogue

Anson

"Thank you for agreeing to come." With her newborn strapped to her, Amara opens the door of a single-wide trailer.

I notice the bracelet Xavier gave her, and Agent Reed returned to her, on the same wrist as her chain of hearts tattoo.

She steps onto a recently patched wooden porch, hardly large enough to accommodate two people. There are plant pots hanging over the railing, brimming with stargazer lilies. The front yard teems with goldenrod and wildflowers. The gravel driveway bumps up to a vegetable garden.

Sidney, the friend Amara lives with, steps out behind her. The addition of another person pushes us into the yard.

"Congratulations." Rae Lee offers, extending her healed arm to touch the baby's tiny hand. "She's beautiful."

"What's her name?" I ask, interested, yet cautious not to act as familiar with Amara's baby the way Rae Lee can.

"Xara. Xara Martin. I'm glad she's a girl. I mean, I knew all along what I was having, but I'm glad for him..." Amara wipes an errant tear away, trying to stop emotion from overwhelming her, "...now that I know Xavier wanted a little girl."

Standing behind the young woman, Sidney rubs her upper arms.

After her release from the hospital, the pair endured considerable questioning by Agent Reed. Facing possible obstruction of justice charges, I'm happy to say both teens were cooperative, and their recounts of the events that night matched.

Despite finding no footage whatsoever of Amara and Xavier together outside of their jobs at her father's gas station, the ISB uncovered video surveillance of Sidney buying a Mountain Dew coinciding with the time Xavier fell from the bridge. He'd also used his credentials for online gaming. When the authorities subpoenaed the company's servers, it showed he logged on and off almost immediately, consistent with what he'd told Agent Reed. Amara had pounded on his door for help right after he'd gotten home from the grocery store, and he was about to play a game.

As for Amara, it was so early in her pregnancy she couldn't have known she was expecting. That, and Amara's deep attachment to her child—breaking down that the baby was the only thing left of the boy she loved, and the regret she and Sidney hadn't found Xavier; believing he might have lived if they had—put fears to rest over a lovers quarrel.

With Xavier's daughter's best interest on the line, the ISB was unwilling to risk increasing the possibility of neglect that too many kids who grow up in rural areas can't escape. With Amara's due date approaching, getting child protective services involved after the baby's birth wasn't beneficial to anyone. Nor would it do anything to honor the victim they'd spent months seeking justice for.

In the end, neither of the teens was charged for withholding information, and Xavier Martin's death was ruled an accident. Moira closed the investigation, satisfied with the outcome.

Sidney offers Amara a tissue. "Sorry, we're not getting a lot of sleep," he says.

Amara blows out a deep breath. "I don't like to sleep. When I close my eyes, I can still feel his fingers slipping through mine." She kisses the baby's tight fist, wrapped in her hand.

Rae Lee puts her hand around it. "You have something to hold onto now."

"My dad refuses to speak to me, but I start working at the grocery store soon, and Sidney's sister offered to watch the baby." She straightens her spine.

"My sister stays home with my niece and nephew," Sidney says.

"That's nice of her," I reply.

"We might not love each other the way we're

supposed to, but Sidney's a good dad."

"Thanks, 'Mara." Sidney beams with pride, like it's the first time his best friend has given him the compliment.

It's good Amara has a support network, and Sidney's still stepping up as a father figure. Both seemed to have gained confidence, removing themselves from Mr. Henderson's watchful eye and going through the ordeal that they had. I don't expect the teenagers' lives will be easy ones. It wouldn't shock me if they went their separate ways. But the choices they're making at the moment are setting themselves up for a better future.

Amara dabs the damp tissue at her face. "Rae Lee, can I ask you how you did that? Channeled Xavier."

"I can't be certain. Possession never happened to me before."

I clear my throat. We came to see Amara, knowing she needed closure and would ask Rae Lee hard questions, but the word "possession" makes me uncomfortable.

"Is he still here?" Amara wants to know.

"No, Xavier isn't here. I don't know where he is, but he's not connected to this place the way he was to your father's service station."

"So, I probably won't feel his presence again."

"I can't answer that. On one hand, I'd like to think Xavier's work on earth is complete. On the other hand, I want to believe, if you or the baby ever needed him, he'd show himself again."

"But you wouldn't count on it." Amara offers Rae

Lee a watery smile.

"No, sweetheart, I wouldn't," Rae Lee replies sympathetically.

"That's okay, I guess." Amara shrugs sadly. "We might move, anyway. If we can save enough."

"My parents fell in love with this little one after she was born." Sidney reaches out to cup Xara's tiny head. "They offered me some of the tuition money they'd put aside and then took off the table when they thought I'd gotten Amara pregnant. They weren't happy that I lied, and lost my shot at attending college right away. But knowing I had a decent reason for stepping up for a friend changed their perspective. It's going to be an uphill battle, but—"

"I think you'll make it," I tell them, because I do.

My lifelong dream was to be a cop. However, in this career, I want better for everyone than the often tragic circumstances I meet them under.

"I understand you and Xavier connected over mutual loss and that your mom passed before you met him." Rae Lee opens a door I wasn't sure she intended to.

When my fiancée and I discussed her interactions with the spirits at the gas station, she mentioned Mrs. Henderson. Rae Lee believes Mrs. Henderson is an intelligent haunting. During Rae Lee's abundance of free time after her fall, she tried to interpret the unusual visuals Amara's mother projected.

"It might take longer to get your degree, but I think she'd be proud knowing you followed your dreams and went to college, too."

"She really wanted that for me." Amara bites her chapped lip. "Do you think there's a possibility she's okay with me not going to the school she wanted me to attend?"

"I know so," Rae Lee says, unusually sure of herself.

"I believe you." Amara clutches Rae Lee's hand. "I was at school when my mom died. I didn't get to say goodbye to her or tell her I loved her. Over the past few months, I've wanted the connection with her I'd felt through you with Xavier. As much as it can, what you said fixes that need. Thank you for bringing me peace."

"You're welcome."

Rae Lee gives Amara a hug, and I shake Sidney's hand before we get into the car to leave. Shifting into gear, I'm glad Rae Lee didn't tell Amara she could contact her again, and that this is the end. What happened during the Xavier Martin investigation left me fearful for her safety. Rae Lee's concussion and broken elbow were the best-case scenario. I don't want the woman I want to spend the rest of my life with losing hers.

In the rearview, the teenagers huddle together, waving. Their decision not to give up on their education reminds me of the resilience of the human spirit.

When I look over at Raleigh, my heart swells. Rae Lee Chatham's calling is hard, but she's resilient too.

She's proven to me she can mend the souls of people who have been waiting for the day their loved ones find peace. And maybe someday, strengthened by her love and devotion, I'll regain the peace of mind I once had, and we'll close another cold case together.

Thank you for reading Mend My Soul! I hope you enjoy the continuation of Rae Lee and Anson's love story as much as I loved writing it! Stay tuned for more Ghost Paranormal Romance Mysteries. Until then…

What will an obsessive alpha like Jake Ballentine, the owner of Sweet Caroline's, risk to stay in control? Enjoy the following preview of **Bleeding Heart**, a runaway bride, enemies to lovers romance!

BLEEDING HEART

Paisley

"Paisley, will you have Gavin as your lawfully wedded husband, to live together in the covenant of matrimony? Will you love him, comfort him, honor and keep him, in sickness and in health, and forsaking all others, keep you only unto him, for the rest of your life?"

The end of the minister's sentence fades, overcome

by the loud whooshing in my ears. Sweat that has already dampened the satin at my armpits and down the back of my gown, making the soft fabric itchy and uncomfortable, now trickles between my breasts. My breaths come in short pants. My heart, searching for escape, is threatening to beat outside of my chest. Not literally, though once a man like Gavin held it cradled in their hands as gently as my husband-to-be is holding my hands.

My tongue darts to wet my parched lip. The underside gets caught on the smudge-proof lipstick the makeup artist applied. We've spared no expense for this wedding. I'd seen candelabras. Gavin suggested the ceremony be at night. And the chapel is lit by candlelight! We are what everyone deems perfect for one another.

Gavin loves me. I love him. How could I not? He's a good man.

But do I not honor Gavin and devalue our relationship by continuing with this wedding? Or do I love him enough to be the "anyone who knows a reason" why we shouldn't marry one another?

keep you only unto him

for the rest of your life

I'd abide by those words if somewhere deep in my gut my shriveling soul was interpreting them the same way that Gavin is.

That's what I have.

A black soul for playing along with a lie until it was too late and embarrassing Gavin in public.

We're in a church, for Christ's sake!

Oh, crap. If I weren't spinning the wheel trying to decide which path to hell the arrow will point me in, then taking Lord's name in vain has added a short, direct route.

Lightheaded, I wrap my left hand over my stomach and bend at the waist. Gavin's thumb presses into the top of my left hand. His fingers pinch into my palm.

"Paisley, are you okay?" His voice filled with concern, Gavin shifts his stance so that he's shielding me from the pews occupied by our family and Gavin's friends and colleagues from the hospital.

"Just, *ah*, give me a sec." The sheer fabric of my veil flops over my shoulder, covering my watery eyes. I try some deep breathing exercises. My chest aches. My fingertips are cold and tingling. Perspiration drenches my scalp.

My mother's compliment from before she escorted me down the aisle rushes at me like a tidal wave. *You're going to have the most beautiful marriage, Paisley. I'm so happy you found a man that loves you unconditionally and that you have a bright beginning, similar to what your father and I had.*

I wanted to tell my mom that Gavin's love comes with strings attached. That he couldn't keep me only unto him, no matter how short our life together winds up being. Gavin needs more.

I can't live trapped in the cage of domestic bliss. I don't want him to kiss me goodbye in the morning and drive away in his BMW, pretending I'm the woman he still wants.

Both of us can't lie.

I can't marry Gavin.

And now that I've made up my mind, I'm in a huge pickle, aren't I?

"Oh, gosh!" I whip my head back, standing ramrod straight. I brush away the layers of tulle resting on my head to get them out of my face. When that doesn't work, I grip the tiny pearl and silver tiara from Sterlings that the veil is attached to and rip it entirely out of my hair. Giving Gavin a wide-eyed and wily smile, I'm positive he's ready to have me committed to the psychiatric wing.

"Sweetheart?" Gavin's gaze is wrought with concern.

"You are going to make an amazing husband." I pat underneath the knot in his silk cravat. "But you shouldn't waste the happiness the world has to offer you on me."

I turn toward the chancel and bolt. My skirt swishes past the altar and I duck out the door in front of the minister's vestry. The corridor leads to the stairs, to the lower floor where I waited to march down the aisle, and outside to the parking lot.

"Paisley!" Gavin yells.

I doubt he'll stay put. I mean, would any groom if they were questioning why their bride left them at the altar? But I don't have an answer Gavin will accept. He'll coerce me back inside and I'll give in so as not to disappoint anyone.

The streetlights above light up the sky the moment I step outside. It casts a glow over the rows of parked cars, highlighting that none are of any use without a set of keys. The limo driver, charged with whisking the new Dr. and Mrs. Gavin Laughton to the reception, is waiting at the entrance of the church. Quickly, I realize I've skipped from one problem to the next. I need to find my way out of here.

"This is why robbers don't wait until the last minute to figure out their getaway plan, Paisley!" I chastise myself aloud.

I lift my gown off the blacktop, ball it in my fists, and start running. My high heels pinch my toes when my feet land on the pavement, making my lips twist. *Shoot!* I was sorely mistaken thinking the blisters I'd have by the end of tonight would be from dancing the night away.

I stop, hop up and down, remove my shoes, and let them clop to the ground. A twinge of guilt hits me. They were such nice shoes. It's followed by a second pang of regret. How can I be sad about ditching Jimmy Choos when I just left the man I was supposed to marry in the most compromising position anyone could find themselves in?

Well, maybe it's not *the* most. But getting ditched ranks up there for embarrassment. Poor Gavin. And my poor mother... *Eeeh.* My mother. I'll find a way to live this fiasco down, but can they?

"Paisley? Where are you?"

"Oh shit, he's still after me!" I squeak.

Skittering onto the cold and damp sidewalk, I pick up the pace. Within the next few blocks, I'm going to go from Historic Brighton to Downtown Brighton to the back alleyways that investment firms thought twice about revitalizing.

Beyond a chain link fence, flashing pink letters on a neon sign catch my attention. Almost out of breath from the heavy layers I'm carrying, I have two choices. I can keep running and risk the possibility of getting hepatitis when I step on a needle. Or I can duck inside and pray that Sweet Caroline's is the last place on earth anyone—especially a well-respected heart surgeon—will come looking for me.

There's a single car in the lot, so I take my chances that the customers won't think I'm part of the stage show. I scoot under an awning, ignoring the marquee advertising the scantily clad headline acts, and pull on a door handle.

"No, no. Don't be locked. Don't be locked!" I dare to glance over my shoulder, reaching for the other door.

Not as heavy as I expect, it swings open, nearly toppling me over. I step into the dark strip club, pulling my dress inside before I can't see anything anymore, and risk it catching between the doors. My practically bare feet can feel the holes in my stockings and the short pile of the rug.

"We're closed," booms a voice from down a dark hall.

"I need to use the phone. Make a call." I arch my spine six ways from Sunday, trying to see in the shadows.

I'm also wondering who exactly am I calling? And how am I paying for the lift because my purse, with my phone and my credit cards, are in the church's undercroft.

Thank fuck I own a boutique because not making off with the money would make bank robbery an exceptionally poor career choice.

A tall silhouette emerges, back lit by the hallway. He uses the top of a liquor bottle to flip a switch, washing the entire theater in harsh light. I cover my eyes for them to adjust.

"Don't you have a cell?" The man demands, accusing me of being an idiot.

A whole congregation agrees you're not far off, dude.

"I lost it." Along with my sanity.

I blink, and the man across the room is staring at me in shock.

Can't say I blame him. I'm sort of shocked about how my night is going, too. Although, I'm the slightest bit more prepared for this encounter than Sweet Caroline's proprietor is.

From the looks of the desolate parking lot, I thought there would be a bartender in here. A bouncer. A regular watching a dancer spin around a pole, too enamored by the woman taking her clothes off on stage to become involved in my little circus act. After humiliating myself in front of two hundred people who I know, what difference would half a dozen who I don't make?

However, I hadn't factored Jake Ballentine into the mix.

No downtown business owner has to have met him to know him. Jake is a man whose reputation precedes him. His omnipotent presence in this small town is as much an institution as the gentleman's club he owns.

More than Jake's questionable dealings tower above. From across the room, he looms gigantic. Long and lean, Jake is dressed in crisp black trousers. His unbuckled belt jangles at his hips. Several buttons on his shirt are undone at the collar. The power in his neck and broad shoulders is similar to a competitive swimmer. His tie hangs loose. His blond hair is disheveled like he's gripped it at the root, but it appears he's also tried to mat it down and back into place.

I'm uncertain if the attempt to make himself look presentable is for my benefit. I would have buckled the belt first, but that's just me, and I'm a girl.

Jake strides over the carpeting with the bottle of amber liquid in his grip. He sets it on a small round table as he passes.

"I thought the princess lost a shoe leaving the ball?"

I crane my neck to reply. "Oh, I did that bitch one better." I lift the tattered hem of my soiled gown and wiggle my toes.

His cantankerous laughter bounces off the walls. "Come on, which one of the guys set me up?" He shakes his head, unbelieving. "I could have sworn Trig and Carver were having too much fun with their respective wives to notice I left."

I shake my head in response. "No clue what you are talking about. Didn't know you were closed. Didn't remember my cell."

Jake plays with the cleft in his square chin. His pupils are wide and black with an icy blue halo. He stares, daring me to hide the truth from him. "It can't be that simple."

"Uh, yeah. It can," I say sarcastically. It is the truth and I'm coming down from the adrenaline high of hot-footing it out of a church during my wedding. "So can I—"

The door flings open interrupting me.

"I need to use your phone. Please! I left mine at the church a few blocks away and I need to tell my fiancée's mother… Paisley?"

Oh, fuckkity, fuck, fuck.

My shoulders hit my ears. I'm caught in Jake's blue-eyed tractor beam, unable to turn and look at Gavin.

"Just go with it," I whisper under my breath.

I jump before even realizing what I'm doing. Wrapping my arms around his neck, the Norse God's palms encase my ass, and our bodies press flush together. Jake plays along, kissing me as if runaway brides barrel into his establishment every single day, searching for sanctuary.

And while this kiss isn't the one I anticipated ending my wedding day with, I have to admit Jake Ballentine is an amazing kisser.

Ready to read more?
Bleeding Heart is available now!
www.jodykaye.com/bleedingheart

Also by Jody Kaye

Shattered Hearts of Carolina
Splinter of Hope
Shred of Decency
Sliver of Truth
Holding Onto Hope
Home Wrecker
Deep Gap
Bleeding Heart
Shattered Soul

Shattered Hearts of Carolina
Ghost Psychic Mystery Romance
Fragments of the Past
Mend My Soul

The Kingsbrier Legacy
Love Thy Neighbor
Gray Sin
Going Down
Love Me Fast
Rumor Has It
Measure of a Man
Never Get Over You

The Kingsbrier Quintuplets
Eric
Brier
Daveigh
Miss Cavanaugh
Cavanaugh
Adam
Colette
Colton

Kingsbrier Love Stories
All My Firsts: Tessa & Alcee

The Canvas Duet
Canvas
Imprint

Author Notes

A heartfelt thank you to every reader who reached out after *Fragments of Past* was published. Your encouraging words about the uniqueness of Rae Lee and Anson's love story were the inspiration I needed to continue writing these characters. I appreciate your support more than you know, and I hope to bring you many more romances featuring a heroine who "just happens" to be a psychic medium.

About the Author

Jody's husband asked what she'd been doing all day. After five years she finally confessed, "When no one is around, I write."

Okay, it was more like a bunch of stammering and trying to get out of saying a thing. Jody's a writer. You want it pretty. Let's compromise.

"Just finish one," he said, challenging her to complete a story and share it. Little did he know that those words of encouragement meant they'd return from a family vacation with a wild and defiant set of quintuplets stumbling their way into adulthood. Wasn't raising their three sons enough?

A native of nowhere, Jody settled in New England for 17 years before agreeing to uproot her brood of boys and move to North Carolina. She's a part-time graphic designer and marketeer with over twenty years' experience, and full-time writer. If Jody ever gets lost, you'll find her reading, all the while hoping that her ravenous children haven't eaten all the ingredients before she's cooked dinner.

To view more great titles,
sign up for Jody Kaye's newsletter,
or find her on social media go to
www.jodykaye.com or

Scan Now!